"I understand you dated this Byron, didn't you?" Mrs. Warner asked.

"His name is Brian," Adrienne said. "Yes, I did."

"Well," Mrs. Warner said, "wouldn't it be nice if you two got back together? And wouldn't it be wonderful if you did that before the debutante ball?" Mrs. Warner continued. "And then my darling Cameron could find someone more appropriate to escort her to the ball. Oh, Mr. Warner and I would be very grateful if that's what happened."

Mrs. Warner placed a thick envelope on the coffee table in front of Adrienne. "That's for you," she said. "Why don't you take Byron out for dinner? Rekindle the flame." She smiled. "If you two are back together before the ball, there will be a bigger bonus for you."

Mrs. Warner will pay me to steal my boyfriend back from Cameron? Amazing. Adrienne reached for the envelope and smiled too. "Sure. No problem. . . ."

BOOKS BY VICTORIA ASHTON

Confessions of a Teen Nanny

Confessions of a Teen Nanny 2:
Rich Girls

Confessions of a Teen Nanny 3:
Juicy Secrets

confessions of a
teen nanny

rich girls

A Novel by Victoria Ashton

HarperTempest
An Imprint of HarperCollins*Publishers*
A PARACHUTE PRESS BOOK

HarperTempest is an imprint of
HarperCollins Publishers.

Library of Congress Catalog Card Number: 2005007720
ISBN-10: 0-06-073180-X — ISBN-13: 978-0-06-073180-9

First HarperTempest paperback edition, 2006

To the doyenne of style—
long may she reign!

Contents

confessions of a teen nanny

rich girls

CHAPTER ONE

lifestyles of the rich and heinous

Liz Braun scanned the sea of perfectly highlighted blond heads, searching for Jane Tremont and Belinda Martin, her two closest friends at school. She had once thought there was nothing more frightening than a horror movie. Now, as a junior at the Pheasant-Berkeley School for Girls, she realized there was nothing more terrifying than the cafeteria.

Even after three years at the exclusive private school, Liz could still feel herself plunged into anxiety when faced with the prospect of sitting alone at lunch. Liz figured this was "scholarship insecurity." The richest and most prominent families in New York City sent their daughters to P-B, with a smattering of scholarship spots given out to those students with the grades but without the bucks or social connections. Girls like Liz.

Liz finally spotted her friends at a table by the window,

and her eyes widened when she noticed the girls sitting at the table next to them: Isabelle Schuyler, Princess Mimi von Fallschirm, and Cameron Warner.

Ugh, Liz thought. *Isabelle and Mimi are irritating enough, but Cameron?*

Cameron Warner. Totally gorgeous, totally loaded, the totally lethal subject of society columns and of most Pheasant-Berkeley gossip. A billionaire heiress, Cameron was not only a spoiled-brat wild child, she was also Liz's sworn enemy. Last week Cameron had done the unforgivable: She had stolen Adrienne Lewis's boyfriend, Brian Grady. And Adrienne was Liz's truly *best* best friend.

What are Jane and Belinda doing sitting near the Billionaire Bitches? Liz wondered as she crossed the crowded lunch room. And more to the point—why would Cameron and her crew allow the merely well-off to mingle with the mega-rich?

"Hey, there," Jane greeted Liz. "The glitterati snagged our usual spot." Liz loved Jane's deadpan delivery, which made even a simple statement sound like a wry observation. A hank of her thick, dark blond hair fell across her face, adding to her sophisticated quality. "However, we managed to score ringside seats for the Cameron Warner versus Mimi von Fallschirm fight." She dragged a French fry through a pile of ketchup, looking languidly at the girls at the nearby table.

"Fight?" Liz said with interest as she sat down. *Is there trouble in Cameron's paradise? Today is looking up.* "What about?"

"Fashion," Belinda replied. Belinda was a tiny bundle of energy, and where Liz's dark hair framed her pale skin with soft curls, Belinda's springy strawberry-blond waves cascaded halfway down her back. Belinda was always on a diet; probably, Liz guessed, because she was totally and thoroughly obsessed with fashion. Belinda joked that she was friends with Liz *despite* Liz's height, long legs, and big dark eyes.

"It appears there is a conflict of interest over who is going to wear what where," Jane explained.

Liz shrugged. "Big deal."

Jane grinned. "Oh, I see. You're less than fascinated by the lifestyles of the rich and heinous because your new boyfriend is one of them."

"I don't know if Parker is exactly my boyfriend . . . ," Liz said as she unloaded her tray.

Parker Devlin was the devastatingly gorgeous boy Liz had met through Cameron. He went to Dudley Academy, the same high school Cameron's obnoxious half brother, Graydon, had attended. Cameron was close with Parker through Graydon but, then again, it seemed as if *every* girl in the Manhattan private-school social circuit was close with Parker. He was that kind of guy.

Liz still had trouble believing that such a hot guy could actually be interested in *her*. According to society columns and high school gossip, Parker usually dated socialites and baby celebs. But he seemed truly interested in Liz.

Jane raised an eyebrow and leaned forward, studying Liz's necklace. "So, Liz, is that little bit of bling new? Did you get a raise?"

Liz touched the Tiffany diamond that was hanging around her neck on a thin platinum chain and flushed with pleasure. "Isn't it pretty? Parker gave it to me last night. It was the first time we've been alone since he came back from Palm Beach."

Belinda let out a low whistle. "*That*," she said, "is an awfully good starter set. I'd say he's your boyfriend."

"Watch out for men who give expensive presents in the beginning," Jane warned. "They make you pay for them in the end."

"Jane, what a thing to say!" Belinda protested. "Pay no attention to her, Liz."

"Who told you that?" Liz asked Jane.

"My mother." Jane picked up another French fry. "After divorce settlement number two."

"Forget her," Belinda urged. "You know how cynical Jane is about romance. Now tell us why you're not sure of Parker."

Liz was about to confess what Adrienne had told her about Cameron's wild party in Palm Beach—the one where Parker and everyone else wound up naked in the pool—when loud giggles erupted at the next table.

"And so then," Cameron said, tossing her perfectly straight blond hair and flashing her perfectly white teeth, "he says, 'No, Miss Warner, I assure you, you will see it on no one else. This is the very dress Miss Scarlett Johansson wore to her latest premiere.' So I said, 'Kevyn, I don't wear *used* clothes!'"

"Who is Kevyn?" Isabelle asked, taking a sip of her tea.

"Our boy at Valentino," Mimi replied, studying herself in a small mirror. She smoothed her already stick-straight black hair and powdered her already ghostly white face.

"Is he hot?" Isabelle asked. Her angelic face, surrounded by golden curls, was a complete contrast to the suggestive tone in her voice.

"Honestly, Isabelle," Mimi said putting her mirror back into her Louis Vuitton bag. "You *would* pay attention to help."

"To answer your question, Isabelle, yes, he is gorgeous," Cameron said.

"And Cameron would notice," Mimi said, "as she seems to be particularly interested in the working class these days. Honestly, Cam, when are you going to dump that peasant boy toy of yours?"

Liz sat up straighter. They were talking about Brian! *Adrienne's* Brian.

"When do you—" Belinda began.

"Shh." Liz cut her off and leaned across the table. "I need to hear this," she whispered. The three girls played with their food while they carefully listened to the conversation at the next table.

"You have to admit," Cameron said, "he *is* cute."

"He's a bore," Mimi said. "Oh, Isabelle, we all went to Town for dinner last night, and he ate"—Mimi shuddered—"with his *hands*."

"It wasn't that bad, Meems," Cam protested with a giggle. "Though he did look like an idiot wrestling with the artichoke."

The three girls laughed meanly together.

"If Brian knew that Cameron sits around making fun of him, he'd be totally humiliated," Belinda said quietly. Liz had filled in Belinda and Jane on how she and Adrienne had discovered Cam and Brian making out at a party last week. Brian and Adrienne had been together for two years, and all the girls agreed that Brian had always seemed like a down-to-Earth kind of guy. Until Cameron came along.

"Serves him right, for dropping Adrienne for Cameron," Jane said.

"True," Liz agreed. "Though I can't help feeling sorry for him a little."

Belinda's mouth dropped open. "I can't believe you're saying that."

"Don't get me wrong," Liz said quickly. "What he did is unforgivable. But Cameron has a way of twisting things around. When she wants something, she can make you believe almost anything."

Jane nodded. "We've all seen her go into her sweetie-pie routine."

"At least I know her well enough not to trust her," Liz said. "But Adrienne was seriously taken in by her. She really believed Cameron wanted to be her friend." Liz stabbed a tomato with her fork.

"It's a good thing Adrienne goes to Van Rensselaer High," Belinda said. "It's bad enough she works for Cameron's family. She shouldn't have to see that boy-stealer every day at school, too."

Liz and Adrienne worked as nannies for two different families at 841 Fifth Avenue. Liz took care of nine-year-old Heather and five-year-old David, the offspring of famed child psychologist Dr. Mayra Markham-Collins. Adrienne was in charge of Cameron's eight-year-old half sister, Emma.

"Maybe I never should have set Adrienne up with that job," Liz said. "Then Cameron never would have met Brian."

"But then you might not have met Parker," Belinda pointed out. "And that would have been tragic."

Liz smiled. "True . . . "

Another high-pitched squeal came from the next table. "Can you believe it?" Mimi shrieked. "Her father offered to *pay* to get her a place at the dance!"

"Can you do that?" Isabelle asked.

"Of course not!" Mimi huffed. "You are either asked, or you are *not* asked."

To what dance? Liz wondered, her attention diverted again. *Is it something Parker might invite me to?*

"Okay," Jane said, standing up and brushing crumbs from her blue-and-white kilt—the P-B uniform they all hated. "I'm late for study hall. Belinda, are you coming?"

"I guess," Belinda said. "Though I am so not enjoying the idea of trig right now. See you, Liz." The girls left.

Liz took a last swallow of her water and got up.

"Leaving so soon?" came a familiar voice from behind her. "The bell hasn't rung yet."

Liz turned to see Cameron's always camera-ready face.

"Why don't you join us?" Cam said, smiling sweetly.

Liz's eyes narrowed. *She must want something. But what?* She knew she should just walk away, but curiosity took over, and she sat down.

"So," Mimi said, "back to the cotillion."

"The what?" Liz asked.

"The Manhattan Cotillion," Isabelle said. "It's a debutante ball."

"It is *the* debutante ball," Cameron corrected.

"You see, every year for, like, the last hundred years," Isabelle said, speaking slowly as if Liz were in kindergarten, "the Manhattan Cotillion committee gets together and they invite ten girls—five from New York, and five from other cities."

"Five socially acceptable cities," said Mimi. "Boston, Philadelphia, Charleston . . ." She blinked. "I can't remember the other two." She turned to Cameron. "*Are* there two other acceptable American cities?"

"Anyway," Isabelle continued, "the ball is held at the Plaza Hotel at the end of January—"

"Giving us plenty of time to recover from all the holiday cheer," Cameron interrupted with a laugh.

"And the ten girls make their bow to society," Isabelle finished.

"Aka, everyone we know and adore," Cameron added.

"You're presented, you curtsy and, voilà, you are introduced to society," concluded Mimi.

"But if you've all known one another since you were kids, why do you need to be introduced?" Liz asked. *The rituals of the rich are so weird.*

"That's not the point," Cameron said, obviously amused by Liz's lack of training in these Byzantine social customs. "What matters is that only the girls from the best and oldest families get invited."

Liz nodded. Now she got it. This was all just an excuse to create yet another clique—another set of "in" girls and "out" girls.

"You know, Cam, I'd be a little worried if I were you. It's not as if your family is old money," Mimi said with a smirk. "Your father made all his own money recently, and moved from Texas to New York, like, ten years ago."

"Sometimes money just speaks for itself, if you have enough of it," Cameron said airily. "Besides, I've got it all. My stepmother Christine's family sent their *servants* over on the *Mayflower* to get things ready, and they're so *totally* old money. Besides, she's a ball chairwoman."

"Still," Isabelle pointed out, "you'll never make Deb of the Year."

"Deb of the Year?" Liz repeated, hoping she didn't sound hopelessly clueless.

"It's *fabulous*," Cam said. "If you get elected by the cotillion committee, you end up with your face on the cover of *Town and Country* and in the *Social Register Journal*. Also, every designer wants you for their spring runway show."

"Which is why *I* am going to be Deb of the Year," Mimi declared.

"Not on your life!" Cameron countered.

"She *is* a real princess, Cam," Isabelle said. "Even *you* can't top that."

"Watch me," Cameron said, her ice-gray eyes flashing.

Interesting, Liz thought. *Something that might actually be out of Cameron's grasping reach.*

"I'll be in Valentino whether you like it or not," Cam told Mimi. "He's making something especially for me."

"Well," Mimi said, clearly trying to top Cameron, "my escort will be Archduke Ruprecht von Habsburg. If the monarchy were restored in Austria, he'd be emperor someday."

This competition is stupid, Liz thought, and wadded up her napkin. "I have to go," she said, standing.

"Ciao," Cameron said.

Leaving the cafeteria, Liz hit Adrienne's cell phone number on autodial. She had to clue Adrienne in on this bizarre new piece of Cameron trivia.

"Hi," Adrienne answered. She sounded down. The way she had ever since Brian hooked up with Cameron.

"Hey, you!" Liz said, hoping that dishing about the freaky rich set would cheer up Adrienne. "Guess who I had lunch with today?"

"Anna Nicole Smith," Adrienne quipped.

"Just as blond, but half as interesting."

"Britney Spears?"

"Still less interesting."

"You can't mean it. You actually had lunch with Cameron?"

"I did."

"On purpose?"

Liz laughed. "Nah, it was more that we were stuck next to each other. Anyway, she and Mimi and Isabelle were talking about a dance they're all going to. And you need an ancestor who came over on the *Mayflower* to get in."

"I know," Adrienne said, and sighed. "Things are insane over at the Warners' with all the preparations. Gotta run. French class."

"See you at 841 later?" Liz asked.

"You bet. I have to see that trinket Parker gave you."

"Wait, Adrienne!" Liz said quickly. She lowered her voice. "At lunch today Jane made a comment that guys who give you presents expect to get paid for them. Do you think . . . " Liz's voice trailed off.

"What?" Adrienne asked. "Do I think what?"

Liz let out a sigh. "Do you think that's true? That Parker gave me the present just so I'll sleep with him?"

"Hello, paranoid!" Adrienne said. "Parker's totally into you. Stop being crazy. Gotta go." She hung up.

Liz sighed and wrapped her earpiece around her phone. She was about to put it into her bag when it buzzed. She looked down at it. There was a text message from Parker:

CALC SUX. MISS U.

Liz grinned. *Maybe Adrienne's right. I have got to chill.*

Liz walked into the changing room for phys ed and caught Isabelle Schuyler practicing a deep curtsy in front of a mirror.

And Adrienne says I'm *crazy?* Liz thought. She ducked into the row where her locker was and covered her mouth to stop herself from laughing out loud.

CHAPTER TWO

the Texas dip

Adrienne hung up her phone and tossed it into her Prada sling bag, a gift from Mrs. Warner. She was certainly the only girl at Van Rensselaer who had a *real* Prada bag, but every time she looked at it, it made her think of Cameron Warner and Brian.

Brian. Adrienne's stomach twisted as she recalled the horrible image of walking in on Brian, on the guest room bed, making out with Cameron. Hands groping. Panting and kissing . . . and then the humiliation and shock of watching him follow Cam out the door, leaving Adrienne behind.

She hadn't heard a word from him since. Oh, she saw him in school, but they didn't speak.

Well, he was the one in the wrong. It was up to him to apologize, wasn't it? To explain, to beg her forgiveness.

Only it never happened. And it didn't look like it ever would.

Maybe he's embarrassed, Adrienne told herself for the

ten-thousandth time. *Maybe he wants to talk to me but is afraid I don't want to talk to him. That's why he's avoiding me.*

Or maybe not. *Maybe he's fallen for Cameron for real. And it's truly over for us.*

And to make it even more horrible, because it wasn't horrible enough, she had to see him three days a week in French class.

Adrienne sighed and leaned against the wall just outside the classroom door.

"What's up, Adrienne?" Tamara Tucker asked as she arrived at the doorway with Lily Singh. Tamara and Lily had been Adrienne's closest friends since she'd started at Van Rensselaer.

"What else?" Adrienne replied. "Brian."

Tamara leaned against the wall next to Adrienne. "I hear you, girl."

Adrienne swallowed hard. "I really miss him."

"After what he did to you?" Tamara asked. She stepped away from the wall so that she could face Adrienne directly. "You can't be serious. Why would you, after he played you like that with Cameron?"

"Listen, Tamara," Adrienne said, "Brian and I were together two years before Cameron showed up, and never once was he ever anything but a great boyfriend. He never treated me this way before. People don't change like that overnight."

"But he did you so wrong," Tamara protested.

"The only thing wrong with him is Cameron," Adrienne said firmly. "She's the one twisting him up."

"But—" Tamara said.

"No more, Tamara," Adrienne interrupted. "I'm sure of this. Be my friend and don't push, all right?"

"Well," Lily said with a sideways glance at Tamara, "I think Adrienne is right. Brian loved Adrienne. That doesn't just vanish. This Cameron Warner thing is only a momentary brain freeze."

The three girls walked into French class. Adrienne was at her desk pulling her books out of her shoulder bag when Brian walked through the door, his dark, wavy hair setting off his chiseled features.

There are still a few minutes before class starts, Adrienne thought. *Someone has to be the grown-up here, and I guess it has to be me.*

Adrienne took a deep breath. She stood and tossed her head back, and then realized the move would be more effective if she had Cameron's long locks. Adrienne's medium-length red hair looked great on her, but was definitely lacking in the dramatic gesture department.

Adrienne walked up to Brian and waited for him to turn and look at her. He didn't.

"Hey," she said. She flinched at the sound of her own voice. She had spoken a little louder than she had planned.

Brian turned slowly. "Hey," he mumbled, fidgeting with his belt buckle—something he always did when he was nervous.

"Brian," Adrienne said more quietly; she didn't want the whole room to hear their conversation. "We really need to talk. Can we get together after school?"

He looks trapped, Adrienne observed. *This was a bad idea.* But for some reason, she couldn't stop. "Just a few minutes before I head over to work," she pressed. As soon as she said the words, she wished she could take them back—mentioning work would only remind him of Cameron.

"Uh, sorry, Adrienne," he said, "but, I, uh . . . well, I have plans after school. Another time, okay?"

Adrienne blinked. She just knew those after-school plans were with Cameron. *I will not cry,* she ordered herself. *I will not cry.*

She flashed him a mega-watt smile. "Sure, fine, whenever." She spun on her Tod's—more castoffs of Cameron's—and hurried back to her seat, humiliation and misery making her knees weak.

Adrienne glanced at Tamara. She could see the *I told you so* in Tamara's dark brown eyes.

Adrienne sat up straight and stared at the blackboard. *Brian is going to be mine again*, she told herself. *And I will make Cameron pay. Big.*

As Adrienne headed to 841 Fifth Avenue after school, the weak December sun was already heading for the horizon. *This weather matches how I feel*, Adrienne thought. *Bleak. Cold. Gray.*

She wondered if maybe she should just quit her stupid job—avoid having to see Cameron, and not have to keep flashing onto Cam and Brian together. She shook her head. *No.* That would mean Cameron won—by making Adrienne run like a puppy with her tail between her legs. Besides, if Adrienne was at 841, she could keep an eye on Cameron—and Brian. Then, maybe she could find a way to win Brian back.

Besides, Adrienne thought as she strode up to the entrance, *the money is just too good to give up.*

"Hello, Miss Adrienne!" Reilly the doorman greeted her as he held open the ornate gilded bronze doors. "Go on up."

The doormen at 841 used to intimidate her, but now that she was a regular in the building, they treated her with friendly respect. She was one of them: a normal person working hard to make sure that the crazy rich people who lived at 841 were all happy, *all* the time.

The service elevator—nannies weren't allowed to take the regular elevators at 841 unless they were with the kids they took care of—opened onto the back entrance of the apartment. Adrienne let herself into the kitchen.

The kitchen that was packed.

Waiters and waitresses were lined up at the doors, and six chefs competed with one another for space to prepare tiny sandwiches, miniature ice cakes, and assemble beautiful canapés and individual hors d'oeuvres. Tiny vegetables were being washed and arranged on platters, and everywhere there was the soft clattering of china and silver.

"Adrienne!" Tania, the Warners' housekeeper, greeted her. The short Russian woman was nearly as wide as she was tall. "Is like the chaotic! Today they compete, and all is in craziness." She tucked a stray gray hair back into her bun.

"For what?" Adrienne asked.

"They all wish for being chosen to be the maker of all the party servings," Tania explained. "The party where Miss Cameron is to fall down in front of peoples."

It took Adrienne a moment to interpret Tania's fractured English. Then she nodded. *She must mean these people are vying for the catering job for the debutante ball. Ugh. More hoopla about Cameron. Just what I don't need.* Adrienne hung up her coat and stashed her bags in a back hall closet.

"Where's Emma?" Adrienne asked Tania as she shut the closet door.

"She with little Heather in hall. You lucky you is come. Soon, they push each other out from windows. Or

Mrs. Warner, she do it herself. You go now." Tania grinned, revealing her gold tooth, and nudged Adrienne toward the door.

Adrienne wound her way through the crowds of catering people and walked through the dining room into the hall. As she passed the living room, she could see Mrs. Warner, surrounded like a queen by her court.

Christine Olivia Warner—called the COW by Adrienne and Liz—was one of New York's most prominent socialites. She and her husband were on the board of every museum and charity, and they were out every night, leaving their children virtually parentless. That didn't matter so much for Mr. Warner's two older kids from his first two marriages: Graydon Warner, the oldest (who was in college at Columbia), or for Cameron (who pretty much made her own rules), but Mr. and Mrs. Warner's only child together was a different story.

Emma Warner was an eight-year-old genius, and it had taken Adrienne a while to win her over. Not that Adrienne was really sure that she *had* won Emma over, but the two had developed a wary respect for each other.

"Hi, Emma," Adrienne said, walking up to the little girl, who was sitting on a leather ottoman by the window and reading a copy of the French newspaper *Le Monde*.

"What's up?" Adrienne asked, pointing at the paper.

"Riots in Marrakech, the French prime minister is

going on a visit to Italy, and BNP-Paribas stock is up," Emma replied, her eyes glued to the paper.

"Big day." Adrienne knew the best way to deal with Emma was to ignore the fact that no normal eight-year-old kid should be reading a French daily newspaper. Unless, of course, the kid was French.

"Where's Heather?" Adrienne asked, looking around.

"In my room with your friend Liz."

"Why are they in your room when you're out here?"

Emma picked up a small pair of silver scissors and began clipping out stories of current events for her gifted teens French class. Emma shrugged. "Heather seems to have had a panic attack or claustrophobia . . . or maybe both."

"I better go check on her," Adrienne said. She knew from Liz that Heather was an overly sensitive kid.

"Okay," Emma said. "Oh, and Adrienne?"

"Yes?" Adrienne asked.

"She might be upset because she somehow got locked in the back broom closet for half an hour before Liz came."

"And how did *that* happen, Emma?" Adrienne asked, hands on her hips.

Emma blinked. "We were playing hide-and-seek. Who knew she would find such a good place?"

"I wonder," Adrienne said, her eyes narrowing. "Such a good hiding place, back in the servants' section, where no one can hear her scream, and in the only closet with a lock on the *outside*."

"I know," Emma said. "Isn't it just *terrible?*"

"I'll deal with you later, Emma," Adrienne said, and noted with satisfaction that fear now replaced smugness on the petite girl's face.

Adrienne walked back toward Emma's bedroom and ran into Liz and Heather in the hall.

Heather Markham-Collins was small and fine-boned, with eyes that always appeared as if she had just stopped crying. And since she actually *had* just stopped crying, they were redder than usual, giving her the air of a wounded rabbit.

"I want to go home," Heather moaned. "If I stay here any longer, I'll have an acute panic attack. My anxiety levels are very high."

"Heather, don't you want to stay and find out what's happening?" Liz asked. She turned to Adrienne. "I mean, what is going on here? It looks like they're planning a wedding."

"Worse," Emma replied, appearing in the doorway. "They're planning Cameron's coming-out party."

"Cameron is a lesbian?" Heather asked, confused.

Adrienne laughed. *I wish*, she thought. *At least then she'd leave Brian alone.*

Emma rolled her eyes again. "No, no, no. Her coming

out into *society*. Every girl makes her curtsy to high society when she is seventeen. To introduce her to her social peers."

Liz leaned in close to Adrienne. "Why would Cameron need to be introduced?" she whispered. "She's already flashed her tits at everyone in New York." The girls dissolved into giggles.

Emma glared at Adrienne. "What are you two laughing at?" she demanded.

"Nothing," Adrienne replied. "Nothing you need to know about, anyway."

"I'm sick of this stupid party," Emma complained. "It's all anyone talks about."

"I guess it's important to your mom," Adrienne said.

Emma rolled her eyes and glanced at her watch. "It's four o'clock. Time to watch *Oprah*."

Emma was addicted to *Oprah,* and Adrienne knew from experience that the little girl would make life miserable for anyone who interfered with her *Oprah* time. Emma stared pointedly at Heather. "Unless you want to play another round of hide-and-seek?"

Heather's eyes began to well up.

"Okay," Liz announced. "Time to go. Talk to you later, Adrienne." Liz led Heather out of the apartment, narrowly avoiding a collision with the oncoming caterers.

"Adriana?" Mrs. Warner called from the living room. "Is that you?"

Adrienne shook her head. Mrs. Warner never got her name right. She plastered a smile on her face. "Hi, there, Mrs. Warner," she said, stepping into the living room while Emma dashed off to watch the forbidden television with Tania in the kitchen.

There were six or seven women in slim, well-tailored suits, all coiffed, painted, and powdered, and each trying to get Mrs. Warner's attention.

"Dear, I'd like you to meet, well, meet everybody. As you can see, I'm in quite a swivet; Gladys quit this morning, and I'm in such a bind, I simply can't handle everything. Would you be a darling and grab a pen and help me for a bit? I just need you to take some notes for me."

It was *Gloria,* Mrs. Warner's personal assistant, who had quit. *If I'm not careful, I'm going to get sucked into doing two jobs instead of one,* Adrienne thought.

"All right, Mrs. Warner," she said reluctantly, picking up a pad of paper and a pen. "But I have to get Emma to her piano lesson in an hour."

"Oh, you are a love," Mrs. Warner cooed. "Isn't she a love?" she asked no one in particular.

"Back to work, dah-ling," a tall woman drawled. "The-ah is so much to do."

It quickly became clear that all the women worked for the one with the Grand Ole Opry accent. She was so unlike anyone Adrienne had ever met, she couldn't help staring. She was very tall, taller than Mrs. Warner, and her hair was carefully styled into a large blond mass of loose curls held together by a great deal of hairspray. Adrienne had no idea how old she was; her face was completely hidden under a mask of perfectly applied makeup.

Mrs. Warner turned back to Adrienne. "Oh, Adrienne, I'm so silly. I've completely forgotten to introduce you. Adrienne is my daughter Emma's"—Mrs. Warner seemed to be searching for the right word—"companion and higher education adviser."

I guess "nanny" doesn't sound prestigious enough, Adrienne thought. *But at least she got my name right.*

"Isn't she just *precious?*" the woman drawled to her chorus of assistants.

The women all nodded, clucked and cooed, making Adrienne think of a flock of expensively dressed chickens.

The blond woman in charge handed Adrienne an engraved card. "Ahm SO pleased to meet you."

Adrienne read the card:

Debi LaDeux
"Queen of the Texas Dip"
Pageant Trainer, Debutante Adviser,
Deportment, Beauty, and Image Consultant
Miss United States of America, 19 . . .

The lower right corner of the card was torn off, so Adrienne couldn't quite make out the year Debi had been Queen.

"The Texas Dip?" Adrienne said. "What's that?"

"Do it for her, Debi," encouraged one of the women.

"Yes, yes," the women chimed together, clapping their hands lightly. "Do it!"

Debi looked at Mrs. Warner. "Ah couldn't," she said. "Unless Christine *really* wants to see it again . . ."

"Oh, please, Debi!" Mrs. Warner said. "Now watch carefully, Adrienne, because Debi is just a genius at this. In Texas, when a girl is presented, they do this extraordinary curtsy. It is like ballet. The girls from Texas are famous for it, and I want to make sure that Cameron can do it properly. Maintaining her Texas heritage is so important to me—and to her father, of course."

Cameron's father had made his second fortune—he lost the first one—in the oil fields of Texas. He had moved to New York ten years ago, with little Cameron in tow. Cameron's mom was a famous supermodel, who had jetted off to Fiji, never to return. As far as Adrienne knew, Cameron got the odd postcard every few years from her mom, but had no real contact or connection with her. Less than a year after arriving in Manhattan, Mr. Warner had married Christine, and she had promptly taken over the "mothering" responsibilities.

"You are just a doll for feelin' that way," Debi said. "But the dip is more than ballet; it's gymnastics, ballet, and yoga—all in one perfect gesture. It says more about a young woman than just that she is well-bred and refined; it also says that she is strong, athletic, graceful, and well-proportioned. . . ."

Is she talking about a girl or a horse? Adrienne wondered.

"Here goes!" Debi announced. She stood in the center of the room and smiled at hundreds of invisible people. She raised one arm so that it was parallel to the floor.

"You have to imagine that an escort is beside her wearing white tie and tails," whispered Mrs. Warner.

"The traditional dip incorporates an escort and her father, of course," Debi explained. "How-evah, for the Manhattun Cotillion, only the escort is allowed. It creates a challenge."

Slowly, Debi began to sink.

Adrienne watched, amazed. It looked as if Debi were standing in an elevator that was going down impossibly slowly. Her smile didn't move. Her eyelashes didn't flutter. Debi just kept sinking. As the knee of Debi's right leg skimmed the floor, Adrienne thought the curtsy was over. But it wasn't.

Slowly, Debi began to slide backward, putting her weight on her back leg as she extended her left front leg forward in a straight line, toe pointed.

"Of course in a long gown, you can't see any of the legwork," Mrs. Warner whispered.

Now that she was on the floor, right leg underneath her, Debi began to bow, her head falling slowly toward her right knee. Then, just as her lips were about to touch her own knee, Debi turned her head to the right and smiled brightly, raising her head and looking around the room.

Everyone burst into applause.

"Why does she do that with her head?" Adrienne asked, clapping along with everyone else.

"To keep lipstick from getting on the skirt," Mrs. Warner explained.

"What the hell is going on here?" a man's voice suddenly boomed throughout the room.

Mr. Warner and his son, Graydon, strode into the living room carrying squash racquets and Coach gym bags.

"Oh, darling," Mrs. Warner said. "This is Debi LaDeux, Cameron's pageant trainer."

"What the hell is a pageant trainer?" Mr. Warner asked, handing his racquet and bag to one of the maids. Graydon did the same.

"Well, Mr. Warner," Debi said, still posed on the floor, "if you and your son would be absolute dears and help me up, I'll explain."

Mr. Warner and Graydon lifted Debi up from the floor, and she turned to them with a dazzling smile.

"Mr. Warner, I am a former Miss United States, and I have worked with the daughters of most of the prominent families of Texas in order to perfect the Texas Dip before their presentations. I train the girls in carriage and deportment. I teach them how to conduct themselves at debutante teas, I teach them to project an image of easy grace and refinement, I teach them the ability to hold up under pressure."

"What pressure?" Mr. Warner asked. "It's just a dance."

"'Just a dance?'" Mrs. Warner recoiled in horror.

Debi stood up even straighter, if that was possible. "It is the Man-HATTUN COTILL-yun, Mr. War-nuh!"

"Fine, fine, fine," Mr. Warner muttered. "Anything for Cameron." He vanished into his study.

"Hey," Graydon said, sidling up to Adrienne. "Haven't seen you since Palm Beach. Why don't we get together for a drink?"

Only if the drink is poison, Adrienne thought. She slipped away from him and positioned herself on Mrs. Warner's other side. Cameron's half brother, Graydon, was a handsome sleazebag, and Adrienne unfortunately had made out with him once during her least favorite moment in Palm Beach.

Adrienne heard the elevator doors opening into the apartment. Then she heard a giggle. She glanced toward the entryway. There was Cameron making out with Brian!

CHAPTER THREE

Grumpus the great

Adrienne's stomach clutched. She clenched her jaw and ordered herself not to cry—or hurl.

Brian noticed the roomful of people first. "Uh, Cam?" he said, stepping away from her. He nodded toward the room.

"What?" Cameron turned, confused. She smiled. "Wow," she said. "I so didn't see you guys."

"Clearly," Mrs. Warner said, her voice grim.

"Bri was walking me home," Cam said, taking his hand and swinging it a little.

Brian kept his head down, obviously embarrassed at being caught making out by Cam's stepmom. Adrienne wasn't sure if he had seen her. She hoped he hadn't. "I, uh, I should go." He stepped away from Cameron.

"Okay, bye, lover," Cameron crooned. She kissed him on the cheek, and he hurried back into the elevator. As the elevator door closed, she entered the living room.

Adrienne stared at the floor. She didn't want to look

at Cameron's smug face, and she didn't want anyone to see how horrible she felt.

"So, what's going on?" Cameron asked.

"Cameron," Mrs. Warner said, "this is Miss LaDeux. She will be your adviser for the cotillion."

Cameron smirked. "You have *got* to be joking."

"No, Cameron," Mrs. Warner said, her voice steely. "I assure you, I am *very* serious."

Cameron rolled her eyes. "Whatever." Then she gave Debi an appraising look. "Can you make me Deb of the Year?"

"Oh, we are going to be the best girlfriends," Debi drawled. She sat on one of the sofas and patted the cushion next to her. "You come sit he-ah next to me and we can get stah-ted."

Cameron sat down on the sofa and draped herself languidly against the armrest, looking at Debi with a mixture of amusement and pity.

"Now, what handsome boy will you be bringing as your escort, deah?" Debi asked. "A beautiful girl like you must have your pick of suitors."

A slow smile spread across Cameron's perfect face. Looking straight at Adrienne, she said, "Why, I'll be bringing Brian Grady, of course."

I would really love to smack that smile off her face, Adrienne thought.

"Is he one of the Midland Gradys?" Debi asked, her eyelashes fluttering with excitement.

Cameron smiled. "I doubt it," she said. "He lives way uptown somewhere."

Now Debi blinked. She raised a plucked eyebrow and looked at Mrs. Warner.

Mrs. Warner cleared her throat. "While I am sure that Byron is very nice—"

"You really need a boy of *significant* social standing, to appear to your best advantage," Ms. LaDeux finished for her.

Cam stood up. "I'll take whomever I please," she declared. "And I want Brian." She looked straight at Adrienne. "Since I have him, after all. Bye, everyone." She kissed Mrs. Warner on the cheek, and slowly strolled to her room, leaving Debi and her flock clucking.

"I-I'd better go check on Emma," Adrienne said to Mrs. Warner, who looked slightly shell-shocked.

"I'll come with you," Mrs. Warner said.

Mrs. Warner slipped her arm through Adrienne's and walked her into the drawing room.

"The cotillion is extremely important to me," Mrs. Warner explained as soon as they were alone. "I came out at the cotillion, and so did my mother and my grandmother and my great-grandmother. Someday Emma will as well." She sighed. "But Cameron has been a bit of a hard sell with the committee. Mr. Warner's money is too new, and well, Cameron has always come across in public as a bit . . ."

Of a slut? Adrienne thought.

". . . high spirited," Mrs. Warner said. "And so, for her sake, and for the sake of our family's reputation, Cameron really has to be the ideal debutante this year."

Where is this going? Adrienne wondered.

"I understand you dated this Byron, didn't you?" Mrs. Warner asked.

"Brian," Adrienne said, wondering how Mrs. Warner knew that. From Emma, maybe? "Yes, I did."

"Well," Mrs. Warner said, "wouldn't it be nice if you two got back together?"

Adrienne's eyes widened.

"And wouldn't it be wonderful if you reunited *before* the cotillion?" Mrs. Warner continued. "And then Cameron could find someone more *appropriate* to take as an escort. Oh, Mr. Warner and I would be *very* grateful if that's what happens. Wait here." Mrs. Warner vanished down the hall.

Adrienne plopped onto a settee, still wondering what Mrs. Warner was driving at.

Mrs. Warner returned holding an envelope. She placed the envelope on the coffee table in front of Adrienne. "That's for you," she said. "Why don't you take Byron out for dinner? Rekindle the flame." She smiled. "If you two are back together before the cotillion, there will be a bonus in it for you."

Mrs. Warner will pay me to steal Brian back from Cameron? Adrienne was so stunned, she couldn't even think.

But only for a moment.

Get Brian back, show Cameron up, steal her date for the cotillion, AND get paid?

"Mrs. Warner," Adrienne said. "You're on!"

"Okay, Heather, inside," Liz said, opening the door and hustling the small girl into the glamorous, recently redecorated apartment.

"Safe," Heather said with a trembling voice.

Liz looked down at the nine-year-old girl. Heather was a miniature bundle of nerves, but Liz couldn't help feeling warmly toward her.

As the two girls walked into the large living room, a small boy hurled himself at Liz.

"Liz!" David shouted, wrapping his arms tightly around her knees, making it impossible for her to walk.

"David, what are you doing home so early?" she asked. "What happened to your playdate with Wolf?" She pried David's fingers off and glanced up. Wolf Stroheim and his ancient Austrian nanny, Renate, were standing in the living room.

"Ve ended early," Renate explained in a crisp German

accent. "It was for ze best. Ve vere just vaiting for you."

Wolf and David often played together, and it had never been a problem before. But now Liz could see that the sturdy little five-year-old was scowling.

"I hate Grumpus!" Wolf said in a German accent. It made him sound very formal.

David snorted. "Grumpus is *great!*"

Liz was confused. "Uh—thanks for bringing David home, Renate," Liz said. "I'll see you out."

Dr. M-C insisted that Liz always accompany guests to the elevator. Liz figured it was to make sure no one made any detours to check any of the private rooms or peer into medicine cabinets. Dr. M-C was a stickler for privacy—she had never even revealed the identity of Heather and David's dad to Liz, even after a year of Liz being their nanny. Liz knew New York society whispered behind closed doors that the kids were test-tube babies. She wasn't sure, but it kind of made sense. She couldn't imagine Dr. M-C having sex with anyone—nor did she want to.

As Liz walked Renate and Wolf out, a bloodcurdling scream echoed throughout the apartment. It was followed by a series of shrieked "no's."

Liz smiled at Renate and pushed the elevator call button. "I think I'm needed. See you soon."

Liz rushed back into the living room, where Heather was trying to sit on the sofa next to David and he kept shoving her off, screaming "no" at the top of his lungs.

"Quit it!" Heather shouted.

"You'll crush Grumpus!" David screamed. Tears rolled down his face.

Liz grabbed one of Heather's arms and pulled her back up to her feet. She planted herself between the two kids.

"*Both* of you, quit it," Liz ordered. "Heather, there." She pointed to the brocade armchair. "David, there." She pointed to the sofa. Both children did as they were told.

"Okay, what's going on here?" Liz asked. "And what's this about Grumpus? Wolf said he hated him. Who is he?"

"Ugh!" Heather crossed her arms over her small chest. "It's David's stupid invisible friend!"

"He is not invisible!" David protested. "I see him, and he's right here!" He patted the spot next to him on the couch.

Liz smiled. *Invisible friend,* she thought. *Cute.*

Liz checked her watch. It was time for the disgusting snack that Dr. Markham-Collins insisted was the cornerstone of every healthy child's diet. The kids seemed to have calmed down, so she figured it was safe to leave the room for a minute. "Shall I get you your snacks?" she asked.

"Yes, please!" David said eagerly. "And bring some for Grumpus!"

Liz retreated to the huge kitchen, shaking her head.

She put the bran cookies on the plates and had just poured the soy milk when her phone rang.

She checked the caller ID. *Parker!* She snapped open the phone. "Hey there!" she greeted. "Did you survive calculus?"

"Barely," he replied. Liz could hear the smile in his voice. "So, what are you doing on Saturday?"

"I don't know," Liz said coyly. "I might be available. If the offer is cool enough."

"Oh, it's cool—that's for sure," Parker said. "I'll pick you up Saturday night at seven at your apartment."

"Uh, no," Liz said, not wanting Parker to see the run-down building where she and her mom lived on the Upper West Side. At least, not till she was more sure of him. "I'll be working that day. Meet me in front of 841. I'll be ready."

"Excellent," Parker said. "Oh, and Liz?"

"Yes?" she asked.

"Wear something really dressed up. Long, you know? It's kind of fancy." Parker clicked off.

Liz's mind reeled. *Fancy?* If Parker said they were going to something fancy, what did *that* mean?

Parker Devlin's father was a multimillionaire media mogul who owned several newspapers and knew the president *personally*. The Devlins went to the White House Christmas party every year, and Parker casually described *that* as "no big deal"!

The White House is "no big deal," but where we're going is fancy? Where are we going? Dinner with the queen?

Liz tucked her phone back into her pocket, put the rock-hard cookies and disgusting soy milk on a tray, and walked back into the living room. She was surprised to find Dr. Mayra Markham-Collins—"New York's #1 Working Mom" according to *New York* magazine—reprimanding her daughter.

"Now, Heather, if you can't share with your brother and his friend, what kind of a girl are you?" Dr. M–C scolded, a terrifying vision in huge eyeglasses and a hot pink shawl wrapped around her large frame.

Heather looked hurt—and extremely confused.

"But, Mommy," Heather responded, "I don't see anyone else. There's only me and David!"

"Don't deny the existence of your brother's best friend," Dr. M–C said. "I don't want your latent hostility toward me visited on *him.* Now sit on the other side of the sofa so that Grumpus can see the TV."

Heather obeyed, leaving an empty spot in the middle of the sofa.

Dr. M–C turned to Liz. "What is that?" she asked.

Liz looked down at her tray. "Uh, soy milk and bran cookies?"

"But I only see two plates and two glasses," Dr. M–C said. "What about Grumpus?"

Liz blinked. *Huh?*

"Elizabeth, put those down. I want to see you in the kitchen."

Liz followed Dr. M–C into the kitchen, wondering what could possibly come next. *It has finally happened,* she thought. *The doc has totally lost her mind.*

Dr. M–C closed the door, turned, and smiled at Liz. "I was good, wasn't I?" she asked. "I should be an actress!"

You should be put in an institution, Liz thought. What was this woman talking about?

"We cannot step on David's vibrant creativity! Grrrrrumpus!" Dr. M–C gushed, rolling the "r" for emphasis. "What a brilliant name for an invisible friend! David is angry at someone, so he gives his invisible friend the very NAME of the feeling he's repressing. It is the PERFECT case scenario! Elizabeth," she went on eagerly, "you must go along with him and pretend there is a third child. Let me know what David is doing with him. There is an incredible book in this! I can see it now: *The Imaginary Friend: Exploring Your Child's Inner Child!* You'll have to take notes to help me."

"Take notes on what?" Liz asked. "It's not as if Grumpus is actually doing anything. He doesn't exist!"

"Oh, Elizabeth!" Dr. M–C groaned, hands on her ample hips. "Do I always have to explain everything to you? Just HELP me for once, will you?"

"Well, all right, Dr. Markham-Collins," Liz agreed reluctantly.

Dr. M-C turned to leave, then paused and faced Liz again. "You're going to be here on Saturday, aren't you?"

"Just like every Saturday," Liz said.

"Good. Then you can stay late, can't you? I'll need to meet with my literary agent for drinks to talk all this over."

Oh, no! Not Saturday! "Dr. Markham-Collins, I have a date that night," Liz explained. "How late did you have in mind?"

Dr. M-C's eyes narrowed behind her glasses. "You would let your social life interfere with your career?"

Liz's eyes widened. *Being a nanny is NOT my career!* she thought.

Then Liz remembered how Dr. M-C had reacted when Parker had dropped by to see her before. "Well, it's just that Parker Devlin and I are both so busy that it's hard for us to see each other," Liz said, hoping Dr. M-C would go into snob overdrive.

"Parker? Parker *Devlin*?" Dr. M-C repeated in astonishment.

As Liz had figured she would, Dr. M-C practically salivated just by saying the name. Dr. M-C was the biggest social climber in New York, and everyone knew it.

"Yes," Liz replied. "You met him here, remember?"

"I remember," Dr. M-C said. "It's just that I thought

that was a one-time . . . well, I'd think that he'd want a girl who . . . I mean a girl from . . . oh, never mind. What were you asking me?"

"What time I could leave, so I could go on my date. He wanted to pick me up at seven. He said we're going somewhere very fancy."

"All right," Dr. M-C said. "Anything to accommodate the Devlins."

"And Dr. Markham-Collins," Liz continued, figuring she was on a roll, "would it be okay if I changed for the evening here and had him pick me up downstairs?"

"I don't think it will be a problem," Dr. M-C said.

"Thank you," Liz said.

"Just give me notes on David's behavior before you go." With that, Dr. M-C turned and left Liz in the kitchen to prepare a healthy serving of soy milk and cookies for a child who didn't exist.

CHAPTER FOUR

those people
are twisted

That morning Adrienne knew she'd be seeing Brian in French class again, so she got up early to try to look her best.

It had been hopeless.

The Warners were all exfoliated, moisturized, Botoxed, and lightly tanned within an inch of their lives. How can a normal person compete with that? Next to Cameron, Adrienne felt like she needed to become a contestant on *Extreme Makeover*.

When Adrienne arrived at French class, her heart fluttered seeing Brian already slumped in his seat.

He can't be gone for good, she thought. *I have to try again.*

She stood and straightened her Marc Jacobs jacket. *My clothes are classier than I am,* she thought, picking a wisp of lint from her Versace skirt. Not too long ago Liz had to advise Adrienne on what to wear to fit in with the Fifth

Avenue crowd. Now, thanks to her high wages and Cameron's castoffs, Adrienne could out-wardrobe anyone at Van Rensselaer. Not that anyone at Rensselaer particularly cared.

This time, I'll make him talk to me right now, right here, Adrienne decided, *instead of trying to get him to meet me later.*

"Bri," Adrienne said, her voice calm despite her flip-flopping stomach. "What is going on with us? What happened?"

There. She sounded completely reasonable. Just a wonderful girlfriend trying to understand her boyfriend's completely insane behavior.

"Adrienne," Brian said, meeting her gaze for the first time in a week. "I just think this is the right thing to do. You know, see other people for a while."

"Oh, come on," Adrienne scoffed. "You can't really be serious about Cameron!" *Okay, so much for cool and calm. But, really! How dense is he?*

"Why not?" Brian looked offended. "You don't think I'm good enough for her?"

Adrienne shook her head. "No, Brian. You're *too* good for her. Can't you see she's using you? You *know* she's not the kind of girl for you. So maybe you two had a fling or whatever. We can still work it out." She looked up at him, her eyes huge with hope.

Brian sighed. "We were getting too intense, Adrienne. Let's just take some time off to explore and see what we really want. I'm sorry if this isn't what you want to hear, but I really think it's for the best."

Adrienne didn't know how to respond. *How can he be so cruel?* For the first time, she wasn't so sure about getting Brian back.

"I wonder where the teacher is . . ." Brian said, glancing at his watch. Its diamond face glittered and sparkled in the light.

Adrienne knew there was no way Brian could afford a watch by Jacob the Jeweler. He was always scrambling for cash. He lived with his parents and three brothers up in Washington Heights, and money was seriously tight.

Cameron sure is doling out the gifts. Adrienne bit her lip. Brian had never been impressed by this kind of thing before. But now, Cameron's goodies seemed to entice him.

All of her goodies.

"So, where did you get the watch?" Adrienne asked, pretending she didn't know.

"Cam gave it to me," Brian said, admiring the shiny watch. "She got it for free. It's killer, right?"

Adrienne put on the disinterested expression she had learned from Cameron. "Watch out for girls who give you expensive gifts in the beginning," she warned, quoting Liz's friend Jane, hoping she sounded cool and wordly. "They'll make you pay for them in the end."

Brian looked confused, then shrugged. "Whatever."

Adrienne walked back to her seat between Tamara and Lily. Obviously they had watched the whole scene.

"I'm sorry, Adrienne," Tamara said quietly. "Trust me. He'll come crawling back to you when that rich girl tosses him aside for next season's man."

Lily frowned. "It stinks, Adrienne," she agreed. "You know, I really thought you could do it. But he's seriously gone on Cameron."

Tamara studied Brian with dark, narrowed eyes. "It's hard to compete with those gifts. That diamond watch looks like it's going to dislocate his shoulder."

Adrienne fought back waves of disappointment. She took in a deep breath. "I *do* have a way to compete with Cameron," she announced.

"How?" Lily asked.

"Mrs. Warner offered to pay me to get Brian away from Cameron," Adrienne said, settling back into her chair. "She'll help me in any way she can."

"What?" Tamara and Lily chimed together. Adrienne could see they were both floored.

"That's right," Adrienne said, ignoring their shocked expressions and pulling her books out of her book bag. "If I steal Brian away from Cameron before her debutante ball, I collect a bonus from the *very* grateful Mr. and Mrs. Warner. They will even give me spending money to put the plan into action."

"Damn," Tamara said quietly, shaking her head. "Those people are twisted, you know?"

"I know," Adrienne said. "Believe me, I know."

Adrienne arrived at the Warners' that afternoon to discover Cameron walking back and forth across the marble foyer with a heavy book balanced on her head. Debi, the Texan cotillion consultant, observed Cameron's every move, while one of her helmet-haired assistants took notes.

"Shoulders back, Cameron," Debi ordered. "Smile! Judges hate a grumpy girl!"

"I'm not a contestant, and there are no judges!" Cameron retorted. The book slipped from her head to the floor with a crash.

An assistant scurried to retrieve the book. She held it out to Cameron, who glared at her and crossed her arms, refusing to take it. The assistant turned to Debi, looking for backup.

Debi crossed her arms too, and raised a plucked eyebrow at Cameron. Neither blond blinked.

Adrienne grinned. *Interesting. Immovable object meeting an irresistible force. I wonder who's going to win this battle of wills.*

"Cameron, *New York* will be your judge," Debi said, smoothing her perfectly coiffed hair. "You are a beautiful girl. You have every advantage. But if you want to be Deb of the Year, you have much to learn."

Cameron rolled her eyes.

"That Princess Mimi has something you don't have. Something that is required of any debutante who hopes to truly make her mark in society."

A flicker of interest—or was it worry?—crossed Cameron's face. She uncrossed her arms and placed a hand on a jutting hip. "And that is . . . ?"

Debi smiled.

Score one for the Texas Dipper, Adrienne thought. *She just won this round.*

"*That* is an easy, graceful confidence that comes with having a secure social position."

Cameron opened her mouth as if she was about to protest, but Debi kept speaking. "Models don't have it. And, my de-ah, you walk like a fashion model. And that simply won't do. You must walk like a queen!"

Adrienne watched Cameron take the book from Debi's assistant and place it back on her head. She tottered a bit on her mile-high Jimmy Choos.

"No, no, no," Debi clucked. Cameron cringed.

Amazing, Adrienne thought. *Someone is actually being paid to criticize Cameron. There's a job I'd like to have!*

"Think position. Think status," Debi ordered.

"You're saying you want me to walk with confidence?" Cameron said, trying to figure out what Debi was asking of her. She was obviously stunned that there was someone in the world who didn't think she was perfect.

"No, honey," Debi corrected. "Right now, you walk like you have confidence in your daddy's bank account. You need to walk as if you have confidence in your family heritage. More like Princess Mimi."

Cameron flinched at being unfavorably compared with her friend. But she sucked in her breath and tried again. This time, Adrienne could see Cameron add a bit of Mimi's regal posture to her usual loping stride.

"That's it!" Debi said. "That's the *you* we're looking for! Now do it again!"

I guess I can't just stand here being entertained by Debi humiliating Cameron, Adrienne realized. She went looking for Emma. The first place she checked was the library—a favorite room for the precocious little girl—and spotted the tip of a blond head poking over the top of the sofa. She heard a tiny, muffled sob.

"What's wrong, Emma?" Adrienne asked, concerned. She walked around the sofa. "Did Oprah retire?"

Adrienne was shocked to see Mrs. Warner rising from the sofa. "No," Mrs. Warner said, her voice shaky. "I saw Oprah in Montecito three weeks ago. Her contract runs until 2012." She dabbed at her eyes with a lace-trimmed Belgian linen handkerchief from La Perla.

"Mrs. Warner, are you okay?" Adrienne asked.

"Not really," Mrs. Warner admitted, twisting the hankie.

"I'm sorry you had to see me have the come-aparts." She sighed and drifted back down on the sofa again, evidently too weak to stand.

Adrienne wasn't sure what to do. The woman had always seemed so in charge. Insane, but in charge. What could be bothering her?

"Adrienne, I have been a chairwoman for the Manhattan Cotillion for . . . years, but *suddenly* there are rumors that I am to be replaced!"

"But why?" Adrienne asked, perplexed. "You're, like, the most important woman in the city."

"Thank you, dear." Mrs. Warner sniffed daintily. "*I* certainly think so. But it seems that people are really opposed to Cameron as a debutante." Mrs. Warner heaved a huge sigh. "If Cameron fails at this, it will be a disgrace to the family."

"Isn't there some way to get them to come around?" Adrienne asked. "Remind them, I don't know, of how they all like you, want to be around you?"

A spark of hope flickered in Mrs. Warner's eyes. "Yes . . . ," she said slowly, nodding. "Yes, of course."

"Well, I'm sorry you're having such a hard time," Adrienne said.

She started to turn to go back to her search for Emma, but Mrs. Warner reached up and grabbed Adrienne's hand.

"You must help me," Mrs. Warner begged. "Help *us*!"

"But how?" Adrienne asked. "What can I do?"

Mrs. Warner stood and paced, her Manolo Blahniks clicking on the hardwood floor. "We'll host a tea for all the debutantes here. Make it *the* event before the event."

"That sounds like fun," Adrienne said.

"Fun?" Mrs. Warner sounded shocked. "My dear, this isn't fun—this is strategy. Now, with Gloria gone, there's no time to hire anyone else. So I will be relying on you. But your MOST important job is to make sure that Cameron does NOT take that Brian to the ball."

"I'm working on it, Mrs. Warner." Adrienne didn't add that it didn't look so promising.

"Thank God," Mrs. Warner said, giving Adrienne as affectionate a glance as she was able, given the fact that her forehead was frozen by Botox. "Now, about getting organized for the tea. Quick. Come with me to my office."

Mrs. Warner hurried Adrienne into her private office, crossed to the Louis XVI desk, and rolled open the top. She pulled out one of her gray, monogrammed notepads and a Cartier pen. "Let's see. The ball is given for charity. The proceeds go to the Foundation for Children Who Need."

"The children who need what?" Adrienne asked.

"Oh Lord, Adriana, don't tire me. They need *everything,* one supposes." Mrs. Warner had returned to her old self. "We'll invite someone from the charity to the tea as well. Create goodwill and all that." She smiled at Adrienne with a conspiratorial glint in her eyes. "*And* everyone will be afraid they'll look *un-charitable* if they don't come to the tea, so we are assured of attendance."

Flipping pages in her leather-bound calendar she murmured softly to herself. "No, that's the Museum of Modern Art dinner. No, that's the nineteenth-century drawings auction. Yes!" She turned to face Adrienne. "Two weeks from today!"

"Isn't that kind of soon?" Adrienne asked. "It's pretty short notice to invite such important people."

Mrs. Warner swiveled around and tapped her pen on her calendar. "Good point." She spun around again. "I know! We'll just tell everyone that the stationer screwed up."

Adrienne stared at her. "But won't that ruin the stationer's reputation?"

Mrs. Warner stared back. Then, finally, she shook her head. "You're right. We don't want to alienate Mrs. Fine. We'll need her for Emma's next birthday." Her eyes narrowed as she thought hard. "So what can we do? What can we do?"

She stood and paced.

"Yes!" Mrs. Warner said. "When you hand deliver the invitations, you'll explain that the original courier lost the invitations and that these are a rush second stamping!"

Mrs. Warner scribbled furiously on the notepad while Adrienne wondered how many invitations she was supposed to be delivering, and how she was supposed to add that chore to her usual responsibilities—including little things like homework, studying, and her life?

"Here's a list of things to do," Mrs. Warner ordered.

"What about Emma?" Adrienne asked.

"What about her?" Mrs. Warner shrugged. "Take her with you. Children should get out now and then, shouldn't they?"

Adrienne stared down at the list. "Isn't this the kind of stuff a professional party planner should do?"

"Adriana," Mrs. Warner said patiently, "we are all part of this family. And this tea is very important to this family."

This tea that you dreamed up this minute, Adrienne thought as she left the office.

"Emma!" Adrienne called down the hall.

"Yes?" the little girl said, sticking her head out the kitchen door.

"Grab your coat!" Adrienne said. "We're going shopping!"

CHAPTER FIVE

there is no Mrs. Fine

The elevator door opened onto a tiny vestibule. Adrienne hesitated, looking around for something resembling a stationery store.

"Come on," Emma urged. "We want to get this done before I qualify for Social Security, right?"

Adrienne followed Emma through the glass French doors that opened into a waiting room. A huge, marble-topped giltwood table stood under an ornate mirror and nearby, a young man in a cashmere sweater sat at a long, granite-topped reception desk.

Adrienne swallowed and looked down at her list.

Go to Mrs. George M. Fine. Order the invitations as I've indicated below. Remember this is a RUSH order. Do NOT allow them to say no. —COW

The young man glanced up. "Hello, Emma," he said, smiling and coming out from behind the desk to greet her.

"Hi, Nick," Emma replied.

He looked at Adrienne. "And you are . . . ?"

"Oh! I'm—" Adrienne began.

"She's my nanny, Adrienne," Emma said.

"Hello, Adrienne," Nick said, shaking her hand. It was oddly cold and clammy. "Can I get you ladies something to drink?"

"I'll have a Coke," Emma said.

"Uh, me too," Adrienne added. Nick nodded and walked out of the room. "You know him?" she asked Emma.

"Sure," Emma said, shrugging. "Mrs. Fine does all my birthday invitations."

"Will we meet Mrs. Fine?" Adrienne asked.

"There is no Mrs. Fine," Emma explained wearily. "There's Mrs. Clark and Mrs. Grey."

Nick came back in and pointed to a glass door.

"Mrs. Clark is ready for you in the Red Room, girls. Your sodas are in there."

"Thanks," said Emma, charging ahead of Adrienne as if she owned the place.

Adrienne followed her into a room with deep red walls. Two desks were lit softly by shaded lamps that cast pools of light across the rich mahogany. Against the far wall, enormous, red-glazed cases held hundreds of invitations—some for weddings, state events, and other important occasions. Adrienne's eyes passed over paper bearing some very famous names: presidents, movie stars, and several of Emma's classmates.

"Hello, Emma!" said a cheerful woman with gray hair and small horn-rimmed glasses. She was probably in her early sixties but had an ageless quality that only money could buy. Her demure navy suit was so simple, Adrienne knew it had to have cost major bucks. "You can't already be planning for nine?"

"No," Emma said. "We're here for invitations to a stupid tea for Cameron."

"Your mother didn't want to be here for that?" Mrs. Clark looked perplexed.

"She's busy," Emma declared, sitting down in the mahogany chair. "She sent my nanny, Adrienne."

Adrienne sat down next to Emma and looked at the pleasant woman across the table, unsure of what she was supposed to do next.

"Well," Mrs. Clark said, "are we looking for something traditional?"

Adrienne swallowed. From the way the woman nodded and emphasized the word "traditional," Adrienne figured they were.

"Let's take a look at some samples, shall we?" Mrs. Clark suggested.

So much paper! Adrienne had no idea there were so many kinds and weights. Vellum, plate-finish, 2-ply, 3-ply,

4-ply. Paper heavy enough to make furniture out of! At Staples, all Adrienne had to choose between was recycled and regular.

Finally, Mrs. Clark's well-manicured hands flew over the calculator. "Let's see. With the rush delivery charge that comes to . . . four."

Adrienne blinked. "Four dollars an invitation?" *Wow, that's pricy,* she thought. *They should consider e-vites. They'd save a bundle!*

"No." Mrs. Clark smiled. "Four thousand dollars."

Adrienne was aghast. "For fifty invitations?"

"No, for a hundred. That's our minimum. Mrs. Warner keeps the rest, I guess."

"She throws them out," Emma declared, leaping off her chair. "I've seen her do it. Can we go now?"

"I guess Emma has decided we're finished," Adrienne said with a laugh.

"She has been awfully patient with all these arrangements," Mrs. Clark said with a smile.

"Stop talking about me as if I'm not here," Emma fumed.

"You're right," Adrienne said. "We're being rude."

"Thank you," Emma said.

Adrienne looked at Mrs. Clark. "Are we done?"

"Yes, we are. And you'll have the invitations the day after tomorrow."

"Thanks," Adrienne said.

"Have you been with the Warners long?" she asked as she walked Adrienne to the door.

"A few months," Adrienne replied.

Mrs. Clark gave her an appraising look. "You've lasted longer than most," she said.

CHAPTER SIX

the perfect pink

The invitations for the tea arrived two days later, as promised. Mrs. Warner stood at the window, examining them in the natural light, as Adrienne waited anxiously for the verdict.

To Adrienne's eye, they were perfect. The crisp black lettering stood out from the creamy vanilla paper, and the Warner monogram glowed softly at the top in a burnished gold. Understated and elegant—nothing like Cameron.

"They're beautiful," Mrs. Warner said. She gave Adrienne an appraising look. "I never would have thought that you would have such taste. Who knew?"

Is that supposed to be a compliment? Adrienne wondered.

"Adriana, because you did such a good job with these, I'm going to give you a real opportunity. I need you to make sure that everyone is doing their very best for us. Like a party planner."

"Don't you *have* a party planner?" Adrienne asked. She

had seen a petite woman with a clipboard and trendy glasses following Mrs. Warner around for the last few days.

"We did, but I fired her this morning. She really wasn't able to get things done the way you and I can. We're such a great team, and this will be easy. Of course, I'll pay you an additional fee. *And* . . . ," she added pointedly, "the more time you spend here, the better an eye you will be able to keep on Byron."

Adrienne thought for a moment. Mrs. Warner was right. If she was involved in the party, she would know where Cameron was every minute of the day and night, which meant she'd also know Brian's whereabouts. She also knew Mrs. Warner didn't want to pay a party planner, when she could get Adrienne to do all the work. Mrs. Warner dropped enough money every week on highlights, chemical peels, massages, and manicures to feed a small third-world country, but when it came right down to it, the woman was cheap. *I guess that's how the rich stay rich*, Adrienne thought.

"Okay," Adrienne decided. "I'll help."

"WONDERFUL!" Mrs. Warner said with relief. "Here's the list, take the car. Oh, and make sure you get Emma dropped off at piano at Juilliard by four. And after that, stop by here and pick up the invitations. They'll all be addressed by then. Thanks, darling. You're an absolute *treasure*. Ciao!" Mrs. Warner left the room and headed for her bedroom, where her masseur waited to ease the stress of the day from her shoulders.

Adrienne stared down at the list. *She had it all ready for me*, Adrienne realized. *She knew I wouldn't say no.*

Shaking her head, she went to collect Emma. "Ready for piano?" she asked.

The little girl looked at her and sighed. "Adrienne, you are incessant in your demands that my punctuality rise to an insupportable level of accuracy. My Technical Pianoforte Seminar has yet to commence at the predesignated hour."

Adrienne raised her eyebrows, then glanced at the book Emma was reading: *Barron's SAT Vocabulary.* That explained Emma's bizarre language. *She's going to do better on that test than I am*, Adrienne realized. *I've been so busy with this tea, I haven't had a chance to study!*

"Sorry, kiddo," Adrienne said as Emma packed her music into her Coach backpack. "Just doing my job."

"It is well in advance of our regular departure," Emma said.

"We have things to do first," Adrienne said, guiding the girl by the shoulder to the elevator.

"And what dreaded engagements must I endure?" Emma asked, stepping into the elevator.

Adrienne looked at the list. "Petrossian, Les Couleurs, and Valentino."

"In an hour?" Emma said. "You can't do it."

"Watch me," Adrienne said defiantly. *What is it about Emma that makes me constantly feel challenged? Remember who's in charge here!*

Emma popped a DVD of yesterday's *Oprah* into the player in the car. Adrienne leaned back in the seat, watching Central Park zoom by as they headed across town. The car soon pulled up to Petrossian, the city's most expensive caviar merchant.

Adrienne looked at her list. Mrs. Warner's huge, distinctive handwriting sprawled across the notepad that Adrienne now recognized as having been made by Mrs. Fine.

Order a kilo of caviar for the party. Don't let them talk you into buying the gray beluga. It's too expensive, and no one knows the difference.

Adrienne and Emma walked into the beautiful mosaic-tiled interior of Petrossian.

"May I help you?" asked a woman with a French accent.

"Yes, please," Adrienne said. "I'm here to place an order for Mrs. Warner."

For a moment the woman looked worried, then quickly recovered. "Mrs. Warner isn't coming in herself?" she asked.

"She is employing Adrienne as her surrogate shopper," Emma explained.

The French woman looked confused, then smiled at Adrienne a little warily. "Do you have explicit instructions? I know how choosy Mrs. Warner can be."

Mrs. Warner's diva reputation clearly precedes her, Adrienne thought. Then she realized that all Mrs. Warner had told her was to *not* buy the most expensive stuff, but that still left a lot of choices. She hoped the salesgirl would guide her.

"Well, I'm not allowed to buy the *gray* beluga . . . ," Adrienne said.

A slow smile spread across the French woman's face. "Ah. But, of course. We are in the market for something a bit less . . . a bit more . . ."

"Cheap," Adrienne finished.

The saleswoman fought back a laugh. "Let us say 'good value.'"

The saleswoman looked in her computer to see what Mrs. Warner had ordered in the past, and duplicated it. Adrienne would pick it up the day before the tea. In a few minutes, Adrienne was ushering Emma back to the car.

"You have thirty-five minutes to get to Les Couleurs, Valentino, and my piano lesson," Emma declared. "If you want me to be there on time, that is."

"Oh, so now we're talking like normal people?"

Emma stuck out her tongue and turned back to the TV screen, where Will Smith was joking with Oprah.

She's right. There's no way that I'll make it, Adrienne

thought. "Excuse me," she said to the driver. "Can you please take us to Juilliard music school?"

The driver nodded and turned toward the west side.

"I'll drop you off," Adrienne told Emma, "and then come back for you. You'll be okay, right?"

"I'm always okay," Emma said, rolling her eyes.

After dropping Emma off at her music lesson, the driver returned to Madison Avenue and rolled to a stop in front of Les Couleurs.

Les Couleurs was a makeup shop that did everything custom: powders, lipsticks, nail polish—anything you wanted could be customized to your own specifications. It cost a fortune but, according to Mrs. Warner, it was the *only* place to go. Adrienne looked at her instructions.

For the tea, we need a lovely pink nail polish for Cameron. Not a bubble-gum pink, or a shell pink, but not a baby-girl pink, either. A pink more like the sand on Eleuthera or in Tahiti—but in May, not July.

Adrienne rolled her eyes. *She has GOT to be kidding.*

"May I help you?" asked the college-aged salesgirl behind the counter. Her dark hair was cut in a severe 1920s style bob, and her makeup was quite dramatic.

"I hope so. I need," Adrienne said, reading from the list, "a pink like sand but not like bubble gum. More like a shell. Or something."

"Oh, man." The salesgirl shook her head, smiling. "You're here for Mrs. Warner, right?"

Adrienne nodded.

"She's a trip. She once came in and wanted to match a piece of thread she had pulled out of some maharani's sari in India. We matched it perfectly. It was, like, this outrageous hot pink with a touch of a gold shimmer. When she saw it, she said it wasn't good enough. 'I meant the *idea* of a maharani's sari,'" she said, in a perfect Mrs. Warner imitation, "'not *the actual color of it!*'" She laughed, and Adrienne laughed with her.

"You have her down cold," Adrienne said.

"What impossible quest did she send you on today? I'm Gina, by the way."

"Adrienne," she replied, grateful that the girl understood the situation. "We're still looking for the perfect pink, it seems."

"We'll never match what she wants. We'll have to make it up," Gina said. "What's it for?"

"This party," Adrienne said, pulling one of the invitations from her purse. She figured if Mrs. Warner was going to throw out half of the expensive invitations, she might as well keep one as a souvenir. She handed it to Gina, who pulled the heavy card from its envelope.

"Wow," she said. "Pretty!" She lifted the tissue overlay off of the invitation. "What's the tissue for?" she asked.

"To stop the ink on the card from smearing. It's sort of"—Adrienne's eyes widened—"THE PERFECT PINK!"

Gina looked at the tissue. "You're right!" she cried. "I can easily copy this color—it's excellent!"

Gina crossed to her machines and began to fiddle with knobs and dials introducing hits of red, yellow, and blue into a neutral nail varnish base until she had matched the pink exactly. "Now *that* is beautiful," she said, holding the varnish out to Adrienne.

Adrienne took it. Gina was right: It was a perfect match. "That is *so* cool!" Adrienne said.

Gina handed Adrienne a second bottle. "Here's one for you, too."

"Thanks, Gina," Adrienne said. "I love it." She put the polish in her bag and checked her watch. She had just enough time to zip into Valentino, and then pick up Emma.

She groaned. *And then I have to hand deliver every one of these stupid invitations. Emma is not going to be happy. And neither will my mom or my teachers. Well,* Adrienne vowed, *as soon as this tea is over and done with, I'll get back on track with everything.*

Even Brian.

The moment Adrienne walked into Valentino, a frantic, but extremely handsome man dashed over to her. "It's not ready," he said before Adrienne could say a word. "It has been the day from hell, and I'm sorry, but it's just not ready."

"That's okay," Adrienne said. "Do you want me to come back tomorrow?"

The salesman looked stunned, then relief spread over his smooth, chiseled face. "No, it will just be a few minutes," he said. "But Mrs. W is always in such a hurry, I expected you to throw a fit."

"I can wait a little," Adrienne said, looking at her watch. "I just need to be out of here in twenty minutes."

He smiled. "That's great," he said. "That, we can do. What's your name again?"

"I'm Adrienne," she said. "I love the store."

"I know," he said. "Fabulous, right? I'm Kevyn, by the way."

"It must be great to work here," she said, touching a sable-trimmed evening dress. The fur was *so* soft.

"Well, usually," he said. "But today, Kevyn is *tired*!" He leaned in close to Adrienne. "There was a *Russian* in," he whispered.

"Is that bad?" Adrienne asked.

"Oh, nooo, honey," Kevyn said, smiling sweetly and tossing back his long, highlighted hair. "Russians are great. They have TONS of money. But this one! Girl, she was working my last couture-selling nerve. She kept saying that she was going to 'Bomb Ditch' and that she needed better clothes. Now, I don't know where the hell she's going, but I guess she doesn't need fur there."

"Palm Beach," Adrienne said, smiling. "She was going to Palm Beach, Florida."

"That makes sense—she was looking at bathing suits! How did you know that?" Kevyn asked.

"The Warners' maid is Russian, and we went to Palm Beach just a few weeks ago," Adrienne said.

"That must have been fun," Kevyn said. "A nice little perk of the job."

Adrienne shook her head. "Not worth it," she said. "Trust me, that family is crazy."

"Trust me, darling, I know," Kevyn said. "Do you know that Cameron had me absolutely ruin a dress last week? It was an incredible beaded sheath, but she wanted to wear these tall boots with it."

"So what did you do?" Adrienne asked.

"She made me cut off the bottom half of the dress," Kevyn said. "She said she was going on a date and the boy needed to be able to see her legs." Kevyn sighed. "Ten thousand dollars' worth of hand-beading cut off and thrown away. So depressing." He shook his head sadly.

Adrienne sighed and stared down at the floor.

"Are you okay?" Kevyn asked.

"I guess," she said. "It's just that Cameron's date? It was with my ex-boyfriend."

"No!" Kevyn gasped. "Oh, honey, men stink."

"It's not the man, Kevyn. It's Cameron. She's trouble," Adrienne said. "I just wish I could win him back."

"Be careful what you wish for," Kevyn warned.

CHAPTER SEVEN

totally Cinderella

Saturday night, Liz stood in the small maid's room of the Markham-Collinses' apartment, fighting back butterflies while thinking about her date with Parker.

She slipped on the Vera Wang dress that Adrienne loaned her for the evening. Liz decided not to ask any questions about where Adrienne had gotten the dress. She had "borrowed" some of Mrs. Warner's clothes in the past.

The deep ivory velvet dress fit her like a glove, clinging in all the right places and skimming her slim hips. The dress fell into a pool of fabric down by her feet. Her dark hair was a perfect contrast to the pale velvet, which was nearly the same color as her complexion, giving her an almost naked look. The effect was extremely sexy but very subtle.

I am so totally Cinderella, Liz thought, grinning at her reflection. She picked up the beaded Christian Louboutin shoes that Cameron had cast aside and that Adrienne had the sense to retrieve before they got tossed. *Right down to the glass slippers.*

Finally Liz positioned the diamond necklace that Parker had given her so that the stone nestled in the hollow of her neck, where it glittered softly.

Parker won't be able to resist me, Liz decided. *I look just as hot, and just as sophisticated, as any of the babes he hangs out with in Palm Beach.*

Her confidence high, she left the maid's room. She nearly banged into David, who was tearing down the hallway top speed.

"Wow!" David exclaimed, skidding to a stop to stare at her. "Grumpus and I think you look beautiful."

"Gee," Liz said, smiling, "thanks . . . guys." She ruffled David's hair and went into the living room, where Dr. M–C was poring over *Psychology Today*. Liz cleared her throat.

Dr. M–C looked up, and when she saw Liz, her expression changed completely, from irritation at being interrupted to pure shock.

"Liz!" she exclaimed. "You look, well, just *wonderful!*"

"Th-thanks, Dr. Markham-Collins." Dr. M–C had never complimented Liz before. It took getting used to. "And thanks for letting me get dressed here."

"Not at all," Dr. M–C said. "Oh, and Elizabeth," she added as Liz headed for the elevator, "since you're going down, can you take out that last bag of garbage? That will free up Rosita for some other tasks."

Cinderella, indeed, Liz thought. *I'm wearing twenty-five thousand dollars' worth of evening gown and shoes and I'm hauling the trash.*

Liz grabbed the garbage bag and called for the service elevator. Danny, the operator, gave her a long, low whistle. "You look like a princess, Lizzie!" he said.

"Thanks!" Liz flushed with pleasure. *I hope Parker will think so, too!*

He shook his head. "Can't believe she sent you down with the trash. That's just terrible." He stopped the elevator. "I'll take it down. Now, you scoot into the regular elevator. Hurry."

"Thanks, Danny," Liz said. "You're the best."

"If I were fifty years younger . . . ," Danny joked. He winked at her as the door closed.

Liz arrived in the beautiful lobby and walked across the carefully polished marble floors, past the tinkling fountain and orchids, and toward the door, where a familiar figure waited. "Parker!" Liz called.

He turned and smiled at her.

Liz's breath caught. His smile was so dazzling, his blue eyes so vivid against his dark hair and long eyelashes, she had a hard time believing he was real. Not just real—her real *date*! In his black tie, with his broad shoulders and clean good looks, he seemed more like a hero from a movie or a fairy tale. *Stay cool*, she told herself.

"Hey there, Mr. Mysterious," she said, walking up to him. "What's the plan for tonight?"

"Nothing unusual," he said, kissing her lightly on the cheek. "Just a movie and dinner."

Liz shut her eyes and let herself take in the scent of his cologne, his nearness. Then she realized what he had just said. She stepped away from him. "A movie?" she said. "You wear a tux to a movie?"

Parker laughed. "To *this* movie, you do," he said. "My parents couldn't go, so they gave me the tickets. I think you'll enjoy it."

He took Liz's hand, and they walked outside. The whole city seemed to shimmer in the crisp December air.

"Your ride," he said as a chauffeur opened the door of a vintage Bentley waiting at the curb.

The car had the lines of an ocean liner—huge and luxurious, painted midnight blue and silver. It was a reminder of a time when cars weren't just cars, they were ballrooms on wheels.

"This is amazing," Liz said, allowing Parker to help her into the backseat. The interior glowed softly with recessed lights, wine-colored velvet upholstery, and gleaming mahogany trim with shining chrome accents.

"My dad collects old cars," Parker said, sliding in next

to her. "This one is from nineteen fifty-two. It used to belong to Prince Rainier of Monaco."

"Grace Kelly sat in this car?" Liz said. She ran her hand along the seat. "Wow."

"Champagne?" Parker asked.

Liz shook her head. "No, thanks." She knew the champagne would totally go to her head and she wanted to savor every detail of this night.

"What are those lights?" Liz asked, pointing to the broad beams flashing back and forth a few blocks away.

"Looks like a movie premiere," Parker said.

"Oh, right!" Liz said, remembering. "That new Lindsay Lohan movie is opening."

Parker hit the intercom. "Cut across to Seventh Avenue and turn onto Fifty-Third, Davis," Parker instructed the chauffeur.

Liz stared at him. That address was the location of the klieg lights! "You are NOT serious."

"Center seats on the aisle, right behind Lindsay and her entourage," he said. "My dad has a stake in the studio."

Liz blinked and worked hard to keep her mouth from dropping open in shock. *Stay cool*, she ordered herself. "That sounds like fun," she said.

As the car pulled closer to the flashing lights, Liz began to feel queasy. *How am I supposed to act at an event like this?* she wondered, panic starting to rush through her.

"You okay?" Parker asked.

"I, uh, well, I'm feeling a little out of my element," Liz confessed.

"Looking like that?" Parker said, raising an eyebrow. "Little Miss Lohan better watch out."

Liz smiled at him weakly. "Right," she said, her voice shaky.

Parker laughed. "It's really easy. When the car pulls up, the chauffeur will let me out. I'll scoot around the back, and when he opens the door, I'll reach in and give you my hand. You come out, legs first, and I'll help you stand. Keep your hand on my arm, look really bored, and follow me. People will shout out questions and stick cameras in your face, but just ignore them."

The car rolled up to the curb.

"Ready?" he asked.

She stared at the huge crowds, the flashing lights. "I guess."

The car stopped, the door opened, and suddenly, Liz was alone in the Bentley.

So this is what Cinderella felt like, she thought. *I bet she threw up in that pumpkin before she made her entrance.*

The door opened. Liz was hit by a wave of sound. *Parker didn't warn me about the noise!* The shouting of the crowd was deafening.

"This way!"

"Look here!"

"Parker Devlin!" a photographer screamed. "WHO'S YOUR DATE?"

"You don't have to say anything to them," Parker told Liz. "Hold on to me and keep walking." He slipped her arm through his.

Please don't let me trip, Liz thought.

They walked slowly along the red carpet, flashes flashing, digital cameras clicking, video cameras shoved at them.

"WHOSE DRESS IS THAT?" shouted a woman with a microphone.

Oh, my God, Liz thought. *They know I'm wearing borrowed clothes.*

For a moment she froze. Parker patted her hand and smiled. She took in a breath and remembered that "Whose dress is that?" actually translates as "Who *designed* that?"

Of course, by the time Liz figured this out, she and Parker had made their way farther down the carpet and the paparazzi were hurling questions at the next well-dressed victims.

Inside the lobby, Liz couldn't stop blinking, trying to get the spots out of her eyes from all the flashes.

"How do celebrities handle it?" Liz asked. "It's insane out there."

"You did great," Parker assured her. "And you looked great, too."

Liz gave him a slow, sexy smile. "You, too."

"Yeah?" Parker stepped in closer to her. He slid his hand around her waist. "So you like the formal me? And I thought you were such a down-to-earth kind of girl."

"Oh, I am," Liz said, fingering the lapels of his Armani tux. "But that doesn't mean I can't enjoy the high life, too."

Parker pressed himself against her. "And I've been trained all my life to know quality when I see it." He leaned his face toward her for a kiss, when his eyes suddenly flicked away and over her head.

"Is something wrong?" Liz asked.

"Nah," Parker said. "Just spotted some people I know from Palm Beach." He took her hand and led her toward the door. "Let's go find our seats."

They took the elevators up to the main floor and walked through the velvet-walled theater with its crystal chandeliers. The usher showed them to their seats.

Well, tried to. Every few feet they had to stop so Parker could say hello to people whose faces Liz knew from fashion pages, gossip columns, and *Teen People*.

"Oh, hi, Parker," a glamorous blond girl said as Liz and Parker tried to get around her. The girl gave Parker a quick kiss on the cheek, but her voice was frosty. Liz tried to stop staring: She recognized the girl from the tabloids. She was a socialite who made Cameron look tame.

"Bella," Parker said. "Beautiful as always." He didn't sound very friendly.

Bella looked at Liz. "I wish you luck," she said, then walked back up the aisle.

"Don't pay any attention to her," Parker said. "We used to go out, and let's just say it wasn't an amiable breakup."

Parker and Bella? *He runs in even faster crowds than I realized.*

Two guys wearing super baggy pants and backward baseball caps suddenly appeared and pounded Parker on the back. Liz knew them as on-the-rise hip-hop stars. *I guess if you're rich and famous enough you can wear denim to even the most formal events.*

"Parker!" they hollered. They gave Liz very approving looks.

"What up, son! Who's your girl?" the tall one asked.

Liz blushed as Parker introduced her. "You take good care of her," the shorter one said. "She's choice."

"I know," Parker said, putting his hand around her waist and guiding her down the aisle again. This time, a skinny, dark-haired beauty blocked their path.

"Parker," she said, her eyes completely unfocused. "You having fun? I'm having fun."

She's on something, Liz realized.

"I think you're having a little *too* much fun, Cynthia,"

Parker said, trying to guide Liz past her.

Cynthia laughed. "Don't be that way," she said, giggling. "You weren't that way in Palm Beach. See you in Aspen, sweetie." She stumbled, and Parker smoothly maneuvered around her.

Finally, they made it to their seats, where they were surrounded by movie, music, and TV stars. Parker introduced Liz to Drew Barrymore, two actors from *The O.C.*, a couple of older actors Liz recognized from the soaps, and some of Parker's parents' friends. They all greeted Liz warmly—probably because of how proud Parker seemed to be having her as his date. Liz felt like a fairy-tale princess.

"Another?" Parker gestured to Liz's empty apple martini glass.

Liz shook her head no. The hors d'oeuvres being passed around by black-clad waiters were delicious but not very substantial. Another drink would make her completely giddy.

The after-party for the movie premiere was being held at an astonishing Asian restaurant, complete with a two-story statue of Buddha sitting placidly in front of an equally impressive waterfall. What thrilled Liz the most was that, instead of intimidating her, the black lacquer interior, the low lighting, and the beautiful people all around her made Liz feel elegant and sophisticated. As if she fit in. She owed a lot of her ease to Parker. Parker was charming and attentive.

Well, mostly.

Parker grimaced as he pulled his cell from his pocket for the third time since they arrived. "Sorry, gotta take this," he said. He left the table and disappeared into the crowd.

A waiter came by and cleared Liz's empty glass. "You know," she said, "I think I'll have another one."

The waiter nodded, and a pale green drink appeared in front of her moments later. Still no Parker.

Where is he? Liz wondered. *Who keeps calling him?* She took a sip of her icy cold apple martini. *Stay cool,* she told herself. *Guys hate clingy, possessive, jealous girls.*

"Hey, sorry." Parker slid back into his seat beside her. "I hate these phone calls."

"Who's bugging you?" Liz asked, snagging a sushi roll from a passing waiter.

"No one," he said, reaching for her hand. "No one who matters."

Liz quickly dropped the sushi onto a napkin. It would be hard to be romantic with raw fish in her hands.

Parker brushed her hand with his lips. "Have you had enough here? The party is winding down."

"I should probably be heading home," Liz admitted.

"Okay," Parker said, "but there's one last surprise planned."

"Parker," Liz protested. "What else could you do?"

"You'll see," he said with a mischievous grin.

They left the restaurant, and walked a few blocks to the edge of Central Park. Parker led Liz to a glossy black carriage, drawn by a white horse. "Your chariot awaits," Parker announced.

"You are not serious," Liz said.

"I certainly am." He grinned. "Get in."

Liz climbed up into the rocking carriage, much harder to accomplish in her stiletto-heeled eight-hundred-dollar shoes than she had expected. She narrowly avoided snapping her ankle as she clumsily plopped onto the leather seat.

Her nose wrinkled. The very strong scent of horse manure and animal perspiration wafted toward her. *I hope that smell doesn't attach itself permanently to this dress,* she worried.

Parker sat down beside her. "Once around the park and then home!" he instructed the driver.

"We don't go around the whole park at night," the driver said. "And I can't take you farther than six blocks from it. You'll have to catch a cab home, kid."

Parker laughed. "I guess I should have checked before I dismissed my driver."

"A cab home is fine," Liz said.

"Well, how about around the lake and back, then?" Parker asked.

"That, I can do." The driver flicked the reins, setting the rocking carriage in soft motion.

The smell was less strong as they entered the park—probably, Liz realized, because they were no longer parked right over the manure!

The stars twinkled in the midnight blue sky. Liz shivered in her light dress.

"Cold?" Parker asked, putting his arm around her and pulling her close.

"Parker," Liz said, "I don't know how to thank you. Tonight was amazing. The premiere, the restaurant—"

"Liz," Parker held a finger up to her lips, silencing her. "I go to things like this all the time, and they've never been fun before. Not till tonight." He leaned forward and kissed her lips.

Liz leaned against the high back of the carriage, feeling Parker's weight press against her, his kisses more and more passionate, more urgent. Liz wrapped her arms around him, matching him kiss for kiss. She'd never felt this turned on before, this desired. She'd never wanted a guy the way she wanted Parker.

Suddenly, there was a start.

The carriage lurched forward and began swaying madly. Parker and Liz rolled apart and *wham!* Liz slammed onto the carriage floor.

My dress! Liz thought in a panic. *Even worse—I'm*

sprawled on the floor! How totally uncool.

"Whoa!" the driver shouted. "Whoa!" The carriage slowed to a halt.

Parker reached down and helped Liz back up onto the seat. She checked her dress for damage. Other than some smudges, it was okay. Nothing torn. *I see dry cleaning in this baby's future*, she thought.

"What the hell happened?" Parker demanded of the driver.

"You two okay?" the driver asked with concern. "The horse threw a shoe and spooked. I won't charge you, sorry."

"Are you all right?" Parker asked Liz.

"I think so," Liz said. "Purse, shawl, necklace, shoes. Yup. I'm still all here."

"I should have you fired," Parker told the driver.

Liz put her hand on Parker's arm. "It's okay. It was an accident."

Parker settled back down. "Okay, just take us back," he instructed. The carriage started up again—slowly.

"Well," said Parker, "I guess the carriage ride was a bad idea. Which sucks, because I really wanted to leave you with a perfect memory of this evening."

"It *was* perfect, Parker . . . ," Liz said. "And we can make some more memories over Christmas break starting next week," she added. The martinis had made her bold.

Either that or the intense making out. *Maybe it was a good thing the horse spooked and stopped all that,* she thought. *When it comes to Parker, I have no self-restraint!*

"Well, that's just it," Parker said, taking her hand. "We can't. My family and I are going skiing in Aspen."

"That sounds fun," she said, looking down at his hand holding hers. She didn't want him to see her disappointment. She had thought they'd spend the two weeks off from school together.

"Aspen is really cool," Parker said, "I wish . . . never mind." He looked away as the carriage stopped in the spot where they had started.

The driver climbed down from his seat and opened the door to the carriage. Parker helped Liz down.

"Let's call a town car and get you home," he said.

"You don't have to do that," Liz said. She knew Parker lived only a block away. "I'll just get a cab."

"Oh, come on!" Parker pulled out his cell phone.

"No, really. It's no big deal," Liz insisted.

Parker shrugged, stepped into the street, and flagged down a cab. He held open the door for her, and Liz kissed him, long and hard.

Leaving him grinning, Liz slid into the cab and Parker closed the door. He stood on the curb watching the taxi as it drove away.

Well, Liz thought, turning back around in the seat, *I*

didn't turn into a pumpkin.

She sighed and leaned back, watching the streets go by in a blur.

But even Cinderella's prince didn't run off to Aspen in the middle of the fairy tale!

CHAPTER EIGHT

snow job

"Grumpus wants pizza!" David shouted, as Liz placed a soy burger in front of him.

"Grumpus is going to get sent to his room if he keeps torturing me with these requests," Liz said.

"He's faking," Heather grumbled.

David glared at Liz. Liz glared back. "I am not in the mood," she warned him.

Liz had been out of sorts ever since Parker had told her about his trip to Aspen. Not only did it mean they couldn't spend any time together over Christmas break, but worse: He'd be hanging out with the same society group he had been with in Palm Beach. She did *not* have a good feeling about it.

David picked up the soy burger and squashed it in his hands.

"Okay, David," Liz said. "That's it. I've had it. You're going to your room."

"But I didn't do anything!" David said. "It was Grumpus who did it!"

"Just stop it! Okay, David?" Liz began.

"Elizabeth!"

Liz winced. Dr. M-C towered in the doorway of the dining room. "Yes, Dr. Markham-Collins?"

"What is going on?" she demanded.

"Grumpus wanted pizza, and he smushed the soy burger," David said.

"Then Grumpus was very bad," Dr. Markham-Collins said. "Soy burgers are very good, aren't they, David?"

"Yes?" the five-year-old said uncertainly.

"Then why don't you eat it, and Elizabeth will take Grumpus to your room."

"I will?" Liz asked.

"You will," Dr. Markham-Collins said in an ominous tone. "And then you will come and see me in my office."

Liz sighed and started for the hall.

"You forgot Grumpus!" David said, laughing.

Liz forced herself not to roll her eyes. "Come on, Grumpus," she said, grabbing an invisible hand and dragging it out of the dining room.

Liz walked down the hall toward Dr. M-C's office. *This will be choice,* she thought. *I'm about to get chewed out for invisible-child abuse.*

Liz caught sight of herself in a mirror and realized she

was still holding Grumpus's invisible hand. *I'm losing it,* she thought, settling into one of the chairs in Dr. M-C's office.

"Elizabeth," Dr. M-C said, entering the room, "this is very serious."

"I'm sorry that I—" Liz began.

"I have good news," Dr. M-C interrupted her. "My publisher has signed on my new book!"

"That's great," Liz said.

"They need me to get them the book by New Year's. They want to rush it into the next season," Dr. M-C said breathlessly.

"Wow," Liz said, wondering what any of this had to do with her. "That means you'll have to work nonstop."

"It means, Elizabeth, that *we'll* have to work nonstop!" Dr. M-C said. "*Together*, we can get this book done. I'll need all your notes."

"My notes?" Liz repeated.

"I need you to take careful notes on everything that Grumpus does. Every little thing will be important. What he eats and doesn't eat. His likes and dislikes. I will need to know everything that happens." She handed Liz a little leather-bound notebook.

"But Christmas vacation starts next week," Liz reminded her. "I won't be able to do any of this note-taking then."

"That's what I wanted to talk to you about," Dr. M-C

said. "I want you to come with us on our family vacation."

Liz's eyes bulged. *I would rather stand covered in honey on a fire-ant hill.*

"We'll be spending the break at my house in Aspen."

Aspen!

"Yes!" Liz shouted and jumped up from her seat. She almost threw her arms around Dr. M-C. Luckily she stopped herself before she embarrassed them both. As it was, Dr. M-C still looked startled by Liz's outburst.

Liz forced herself to calm down. "Aspen. Notes, sure. I can do that."

"Have your mother call me," Dr. M-C continued. "I hope it will be fine."

Mom. Right. I have to get Mom to agree to this, Liz worried. *She'll hate my being away for Christmas.* She pushed the idea from her mind. "I'm sure it will be, Dr. Markham-Collins. Don't worry."

Liz left the office and floated through the apartment on cloud nine. *I have to call Parker!* She reached for her cell and then changed her mind. *I'll save it to tell him in person on our date tomorrow,* she decided. *He'll be so excited!*

Liz yanked open the door of her Upper West Side apartment building and dashed inside as if she were crossing the finish line at the Olympics.

I can't believe I'm going to Aspen at the end of the week!

The elevator opened onto the florescent-lit hallway with its endless row of beige-painted doors. It was quite a contrast to 841 Fifth Avenue, where she spent so much of her time. She let herself into Apartment 12B.

The apartment wasn't as fancy or sparkling clean as Dr. M-C's, but it was a lot more homey and comfortable. Bookcases lined the living room walls, and the worn sofa was a cozy spot for naps. Even the lighting felt softer and friendlier.

"Mom? Are you here?" Liz called.

"Liz? That you?" Liz's mother stepped out of her bedroom. "Hi, honey!" She crossed over and gave her daughter a hug and a kiss. "I can't believe we're both home—we never seem to overlap anymore."

Linda Braun worked as a real estate broker for a big firm and, as a result, she worked really erratic hours. Sometimes she was free for days, and other times when she was working with clients, she seemed to barely get home at all. Ever since the divorce a few years ago, Liz's mom tried to make sure that they had dinner together every day. Once Liz started working for Dr. Markham-Collins, that wasn't really possible anymore.

"I ordered Chinese," her mom said, pointing to the white takeout containers on the kitchen table. "You're just in time."

Liz smiled. "Sounds great," she said, folding herself

into her usual chair. She waited until they had both finished an egg roll, then she took a deep breath. "Mom, I need to ask you for a favor."

"Shoot," Ms. Braun said.

"I need permission to do something really cool," Liz began.

"When you say that, I hear, 'I need permission to do something really expensive,'" Ms. Braun said, smiling.

"No, it won't cost you anything!" Liz said. "Dr. Markham-Collins has asked me to go with her, David, and Heather to Aspen over Christmas break."

"Oh, Liz, honey, I don't know," Ms. Braun replied. "I know how important your job is to you, and even I have to admit that Aspen sounds great, but for *Christmas*?"

Liz, knowing that being away for the holiday would bother her mom, had already come up with a plan. "What if I go for only the first week? That way, I'll help Dr. Markham-Collins and still get back in time to spend Christmas and New Year's with you."

Her mother's frown softened, just a little. "I don't know. Shouldn't Dr. Markham-Collins really take someone more . . . grown up?"

"I can handle it!" Liz exclaimed.

She watched as her mother silently spooned chicken and broccoli onto her plate. She knew her mom was thinking, and she knew from experience that pressuring her was definitely not the way to go. Liz could always wheedle things out of her dad, but he moved with his new wife to New Jersey last year. Now it was just Liz and her mom.

She ate her food slowly—and waited.

"Liz," her mother said finally, "I understand that you're growing up, and you want to take advantage of the opportunities offered you . . ."

Liz could feel her mother wavering. *If I can just keep quiet, she'll let me go,* Liz thought.

"But I just have one question," her mom said.

"Sure," Liz said. "What?"

"Do the Devlins have a place in Aspen?" She took a sip of her tea and looked at Liz over the lip of her cup.

Busted, Liz thought. *There's no way she'll let me go.*

"Yes," Liz replied. "They do." She sighed in frustration and leaned back in her chair, defeated.

Ms. Braun smiled. "Liz, I didn't say you couldn't go. I just want you to know that I'm not stupid. I was a teenager once, too." She put down her teacup.

"But, Liz, I want you to remember that you have been asked to Aspen to work. Taking care of children in an environment where there is a lot of physical activity is a big responsibility. You have to be on your toes when little kids ski or skate or even walk down a crowded street in a town you don't know as well as you know New York."

Liz perked up. This was beginning to sound promising.

"You can go, Liz, as long as Dr. Markham-Collins agrees to get you home for Christmas. But remember—you are there to take care of Heather and David, not to have a romantic vacation with Parker. I want you to promise me that you will act responsibly."

Liz shrieked and ran around the table, throwing her arms around her mother's neck. "Thank you!" she said, "Thank you, thank you, thank you! You are the coolest!"

"You got that right!" Her mom laughed.

I've got to tell Adrienne! Liz grabbed her phone and texted:

GOING 2 ASPEN

Adrienne texted back:

SNOWED YR MOM?

Liz smiled and texted:

AVALANCHE!

The next day at school, Liz thought she'd burst by lunchtime when she could finally tell Belinda and Jane her fantastic news.

Liz plunked down her tray and declared: "Guess who is going to Aspen over Christmas break?"

Jane looked up at her. "The coven?" she asked, nodding toward Isabelle, Mimi, and Cameron, who sat at the next table, poring over a *Town and Country* magazine.

"No," Liz declared, taking her seat as if she were a queen. "I am."

Belinda's mouth dropped open. "You are so lucky! I have four generations of relatives descending for the holidays."

"Your media magnate taking you?" Jane asked with a grin.

"No!" Liz smiled and tossed a French fry at her friend. Jane ducked and laughed. "I'm going to take care of David and Heather."

"I hear Grumpus is a real klutz on the slopes," Jane teased. "You'll need to keep an especially close eye on him."

"You should be on Comedy Central," Liz said.

"You're going to Aspen for break?" Isabelle called from the next table.

"Yes," Liz answered, not really wanting to get into it with the Terrible Trio.

"When will you be there?" Cameron asked.

"Just the first week," she said. "I'll be home for Christmas."

"Oh, you'll miss the Red and White Ball," Mimi said.

"What's the Red and White Ball?" Liz asked.

"The most exclusive event in Aspen," Mimi explained. "It's always the Saturday after Christmas."

"It's a blast—everyone wears red and white. It is *so* Santa," Cameron said.

"Don't you think Parker will look totally adorable in red and white?" Isabelle said.

"I have an idea," Cameron told Isabelle. "You should wear all red, and he should wear all white. Much more chic."

"Parker?" Liz blinked. "Parker Devlin?"

Isabelle smiled at Liz. "Of course. He's my date. Didn't he tell you?"

Liz smiled back. "Right. Of course he is."

And of course I'm a complete idiot.

CHAPTER NINE

viva Valentino!

After school, Liz walked quickly through Central Park, her mind whirling.

I never should have assumed that Parker would be going out only with me, she thought. *I knew his reputation before we started seeing each other. Besides, that whole crowd mixes and matches with the abandon of a* Vogue *stylist on an unlimited budget.*

She shoved her hands deeper into the pockets of her parka and shivered, as much from frustration as from the cold December air.

All those calls during the after-party the night of the movie premiere, she thought. *They must have been from Isabelle!*

Liz walked across the back of the Metropolitan Museum of Art, along the paths that led to Cleopatra's Needle, an Egyptian obelisk dropped onto a green hill in Central Park. Whenever she passed it, it reminded her of their incredible first date at the Metropolitan when Parker kissed her in front of the Egyptian Temple of Dendur.

Did he kiss Isabelle there too? she wondered miserably. *He probably* did it *with her,* she realized.

She looked up to see Parker loping across the grass, already smiling at her.

"Hey, there," he greeted her, throwing his arms around her shoulders and giving her a playful peck on the ear.

Liz couldn't kiss him back—she was just too confused. He stepped away from her. "You okay?" he asked, puzzled. "You look seriously serious!"

I can't fake it, Liz realized. *I have to tell him that I know.*

"I just want you to know that, well, I'm going to be in Aspen during vacation, and I was telling some friends—" she began.

Parker's face brightened. "That totally rocks! Where are you staying?" He didn't give her a chance to answer— he just began pacing and tossing out ideas rapid-fire. "It will be so excellent! We can go skiing, and I'll take you to the Caribou Club—that place is killer. You and your mom will want to shop—most women do there."

"I'm not going with my mom, Parker," Liz explained. "I'm going to be there to take care of David and Heather."

"Even better," Parker said, grinning. "If you're there with the doc, you'll be able to slip out at night and no one will even know. Doesn't that sound good?" he asked, slipping his hands around her waist and pulling her into him. "When are you leaving?" he asked.

"This weekend, and I'll be there until the Sunday before Christmas," she said.

"That's plenty of time for fun," Parker said.

"I-I hear there's even more fun after I leave," Liz said, nervous about where the conversation was about to go.

Parker looked confused. "What do you mean?"

"I hear there's a big dance on Saturday night after Christmas," Liz said.

"Yeah," he replied. "It's no big deal."

"But you're going with Isabelle, right?" The second she said it, Liz wanted the take the words back. Had she pushed too far? Was she being too possessive?

"Liz," he said, taking her hand. "It doesn't mean any-thing. She's my dad's business partner's daughter. It's a family obligation. And the Red and White Ball is a drag. Even if I had known you were going to be there and asked you, you wouldn't want to go." He brushed his hand against her cheek and smiled at her encouragingly. "It's not your kind of thing, Liz. That's one of the reasons I like you so much. You're so down-to-earth. You're not caught up in the whole society thing. . . ."

Yeah, Liz thought. *I'm so non-society, you thought you could take someone else to that dance and I would never hear about it.*

"Liz," he said, beginning to sound exasperated. "You aren't even going to *be* there for the ball. I'm expected to go, and I'm expected to go *with* someone. That's it."

Liz felt his strong arms around her. He began to kiss her neck, sending tingles through her entire body. "Okay," she said. "You're very persuasive."

"I know," Parker said, grinning. "I'm irresistible."

———

Who are *all these people?* Adrienne thought, forcing her way up Madison Avenue on Saturday morning.

The streets were jammed with what seemed like thousands of holiday shoppers, all determined to wedge themselves between her and the luxurious Valentino shop.

The day of the tea had arrived, and Adrienne had already been sent on several last-minute errands. Mrs. Warner had insisted Adrienne meet up with them at Valentino that morning—probably to get further instructions.

The moment Adrienne ran into the shop, a harried saleswoman rushed at her.

"The Warners are in the back," she said, helping Adrienne out of her coat quickly. "Kevyn is losing his mind. It is an absolute disaster."

Uh-oh, Adrienne thought. *What can be going on back there?*

Adrienne braced herself and entered the room where Cameron was having a last-minute fitting. Mrs. Warner stood in a corner on her cell phone, shouting instructions to the caterer back at the apartment. Emma sat on a small chair in the corner reading *Advanced SAT Vocabulary*. Cameron stood on a platform in the middle of the room surrounded by women plucking and pinning her dress.

She looked extraordinary. The cream cashmere dress was carefully fitted to her body, and stopped at a decorous mid-calf length. The tiniest pink ribbon trimmed the bateau neckline, and a cropped cashmere jacket trimmed in pink ribbon covered her shoulders.

"I told you I look like a nun," Cameron said, disgusted. "Can't you take this dress up and show more leg?"

"Valentino wouldn't hear of it," Kevyn said firmly. "It would ruin the proportions of the dress. This is a debutante tea gown, not a cocktail dress."

"He's right, Cameron," Mrs. Warner said, interrupting herself on the phone. "It wouldn't be appropriate."

"Look," Cameron said, exasperated, "I *know* fashion. I have been in, like, *three* fashion shows. This dress is too long."

Kevyn folded his arms and stared Cameron down. "Miss Warner," he said evenly, "I wouldn't want to question your *expertise*. But I will not alter this dress."

Mrs. Warner flipped her phone shut. "Cameron!" she scolded. "This conversation is OVER. Put on your street clothes and let these people finish the alterations. You have David Barrett coming to the house in an hour to blow out your hair, and the makeup artist *Vogue* recommended will be there right after. The tea is THIS AFTERNOON!"

Adrienne thought she could actually see Mrs. Warner's veins popping out despite the Botox.

"I still hate this dress," Cameron said, taking off the luxurious jacket and tossing it onto a nearby chair. "And those people can wait if we run late."

She unzipped the dress and stepped out of it, dropping it onto the platform. She crossed to the rack wearing only her panties and bra. The women gasped as Cameron's pointy-toed shoe crushed the delicate ribbon on the bodice.

"You'll press that for me, won't you, darling?" Cameron said, smiling at Kevyn.

"Of course, Miss Warner," he said, his voice taut and his smile grim.

"Enough, Cameron. We're going," Mrs. Warner ordered as Cameron slipped her regular dress on over her head. "Emma, you'll come with us."

Emma stood and, never taking her eyes off her book, left the fitting room to wait in the store.

Mrs. Warner turned to Adrienne. "Adriana. You wait here for them to finish the alterations."

Cameron tossed her hair and picked up her hot-pink Louis Vuitton purse. "Thanks, Adrienne. Now I can meet Brian for a quick lunch. Ciao!" She left the fitting room.

"You will NOT meet that boy for lunch! You have a million things to do!" Mrs. Warner said, charging out after Cameron.

"Yes, I will!" Cameron shouted.

"The tea is in just a few hours!" Mrs. Warner yelled back. They continued their argument out the doors and onto Madison Avenue, Emma ordering them to be quiet so she could memorize her words.

"Ladies," Kevyn announced to the seamstresses, "you all deserve a break. Finish the alterations for Miss Warpath when you get back."

The women left the room, and Kevyn sat down, furious. "What is her damage?" he asked.

"I don't know," Adrienne admitted. Her lip trembled.

"Are you okay, doll?" Kevyn asked, picking up a bottle of Gerolsteiner water from the tray that had been brought in for Cameron and her mother. He poured a glass and handed it to Adrienne.

"The way I feel right now, I can't even drink this water, let alone pronounce it," Adrienne said, handing it back to him.

"Rejecting the hottest German water?" He smiled at her. "It MUST be bad."

"Miss Warpath, as you call her, stole my boyfriend, Kevyn. She's going to meet him for lunch, and then throw him in my face while I serve drinks to her friends this afternoon at her debutante tea, which," she added, "I busted my butt organizing."

"Utmost sympathy, darling," he said, clucking. "Let's trade this water in for a glass of wine instead."

Adrienne smiled. "Uh, Kevyn," she said as he crossed to a cobalt wall unit that turned out to be a refrigerator and pulled out a bottle, "I'm in high school."

"Ugh, all the more reason," Kevyn said, pouring a glass of white wine. "Adolescence is the worst. Trust me, I know." He handed her the glass and sat on a settee across from her. "Vent all to Kevyn."

"It just seems that there is no way for me to get him back," Adrienne confessed, sitting on one of the small chairs. "Cam is gorgeous. Cam is rich." She took a sip of the chilled pinot grigio. "Cam's got the makeup artists, the hairdresser, and"—she looked around the fitting room—"and the VALENTINO, for God's sake."

"Miss Cameron doesn't have *all* the Valentino," Kevyn said, smiling. "Wait here."

Adrienne took another sip of the wine while she wondered what Kevyn was up to. He returned a moment later with a large garment bag.

"This," he said, "is for you. To *borrow*," he added with a grin. "I really need it back tomorrow."

Adrienne carefully unzipped the bag and gasped. Inside was an incredible red crepe dress with a short tapered skirt and exquisite seaming.

"Oh, my God," Adrienne said. "That's gorgeous."

"It will look great on you, and you'll *really* love this part." He glanced around as if he was afraid he'd be overheard. "This is the dress Cameron *really* wanted. We got it in right before the fitting."

"Why didn't she take it?" Adrienne asked.

"Because she was rude one too many times to my best fitter. Besides, her mother would have decreed it too short." He removed the dress from the garment bag.

"It is unbelievably stunning," Adrienne said, almost afraid to touch the delicate fabric.

"Wear it today and you'll really piss her off," Kevyn said. "And if you can't get the boyfriend back in that dress, well, you didn't want him in the first place. Just call me your fairy godmother."

"Wow, Kevyn, thanks!" Adrienne said.

"Adrienne," Kevyn added, "I'm serious. I know I'm a dizzy queen selling Valentino, but I know a lot about people from this job. A man doesn't fall in love with dresses and jewelry—he falls in love with the woman in them. If Cameron Warner is nothing but a glamorous doll to your boyfriend, he'll get tired of her real fast. Lord knows I have." He smiled. "Now hop into that dress—you have some serious jealousy and regret to cause!"

CHAPTER TEN

Cameron's latest boy toy

When the elevator doors opened onto the Warners' kitchen, Adrienne realized the enormity of the event that was about to take place.

Florists were delivering dozens of bouquets; huge hot-water pots and chafing dishes covered every available surface; caterers and waiters were scurrying back and forth setting things up.

Tania came into the kitchen and beamed, displaying her gold tooth. "Miss Adrienne, you looking for a million dollars!"

"Thanks, Tania," Adrienne said. Adrienne caught a glimpse of herself in an ornate gilded hallway mirror. *Kevyn was right: Brian won't be able to resist me looking like this!* The draping emphasized every curve, and the red color made her eyes sparkle.

Debi appeared in a cloud of perfume. "Is the enti-yah staff assembled?" she asked.

"Yes," Tania said.

"Aren't you all just PRECIOUS with a capital 'P'?" Debi said, moving toward the head waiter. "Nah, ah want yuh ta know that every GAW-jus, drippy, tasty, yummy treat you have, y'all jes' bring 'em out and serve 'um up, y'hear me?" She smiled for one moment, then dropped the expression and her accent completely. "But you serve them to the *other* girls. Cameron Warner is to receive *nothing*. Keep the food away from her, and make sure that every other girl has a handfull of things to eat and drink at every minute of the party—no napkins. I want those girls with mouths full and sticky fingers. You got me?" She glared threateningly at the crowd.

They stood silently, eyes wide open.

"Great!" Debi said. "Ahre we all clear? Let's get this tea staw-ted!" She clapped her hands, and the workers dispersed.

"Adriana?" a voice called from the back of the apartment. It was Mrs. Warner—Adrienne could hear her shoes approaching on the marble floor.

Here we go, Adrienne thought.

"I just have one quick question for you," Mrs. Warner said, sidling up to her. "Have you gotten rid of that boy yet?" she whispered.

"Not yet, Mrs. Warner," Adrienne replied. "I hope to really make some progress today."

Mrs. Warner raised a skeptical eyebrow, then frowned. "All right. If that's the best you can do."

An hour later, Mrs. Warner's living room was full. At every table, Manhattan's most important women were chatting and talking with one another as if they had no cares in the world.

Actually, thought Adrienne, *they really do have no cares in the world.* And with such power, money, and no worries, the women had no problem making remarks that Adrienne never would have even considered uttering in public.

"She's dreadful," one woman said, putting down a canapé and picking up her tea. "Ever since she fell in with that Kabbalah trend, she's always trying to make me do addition and read all this spiritual nonsense. As if I'm not spiritual! Why, twenty years ago my husband and I were married at that little church down the street. What's its name, darling?"

"Saint Tropez?" replied another woman.

"Saint Thomas," said her daughter, embarrassed.

Adrienne watched the waiters circulating the room.

"Miniature pecan pie?" one of them asked Isabelle.

"No, thank you," Isabelle said, and started to turn back to Mrs. Bleecker, head of the Cotillion Refreshments Committee.

"They uh SO good, DAW-lin'!" Debi said, coming up behind her, plucking the sweet off the silver tray and handing it to Isabelle without a napkin. "They uh di-VINE with cream!" She plopped a towering dollop of cream onto the little pie with a silver spoon.

Isabelle looked helpless as she tried to maneuver the sticky dessert from one hand to another.

"Isabelle, have you met Mrs. Van Tassel?" Mrs. Bleecker asked.

"No, I haven't," Isabelle said, searching desperately for a napkin to wipe her hand. "I'm sorry," she said, her hands covered with dessert. "I'm a bit of a mess."

"Oh, you're just like me," the portly Mrs. Van Tassel said. "You can't resist a sweet!"

"Ladies! A photo, please!" A photographer held up a camera.

Mrs. Van Tassel pulled Isabelle closer, making the cream slide off the pie and onto her dress. The photographer snapped a quick picture; Isabelle looked furious, her soft silk dress stained with cream, her hands full of crumbling dessert.

From what Adrienne could tell, Mimi was the undisputed star of the tea. All the girls stared with jealousy at the Chanel tea dress Karl Lagerfeld had made for her, and at the handsome archduke at her side. The gorgeous young couple smiled and spoke to everyone, greeting people as if they were related to the British Royal Family, which, of course, they were—even if only distantly.

Mimi smiled and fluttered around her archduke, successfully avoiding the slippery and precarious canapés Debi kept trying to put in her path. Her escort, Adrienne noted, gulped down the champagne, but he didn't show it; he just got very pink.

"Princess von Fallschirm is *quite* extraordinary," Mrs. Bleecker said approvingly. "She has adjusted to America and New York so well. Not a rough edge on her. She really is every inch a princess."

"Well, Cameron may have *had* a few rough edges once," Mrs. Warner said with a nervous laugh. "But look at her now!" Mrs. Warner gestured toward the living room.

Cameron stood in the doorway, looking beautiful in her modest Valentino, making a very calculated and effective late entrance.

You have to hand it to her, Adrienne thought. *She looks great.*

Cameron walked in slowly, as if one of Emma's enormous dictionaries were on her head. "Thank you so much for coming," she greeted Mrs. Bleecker in a low and perfectly modulated voice.

Cameron looked at Adrienne, and her eyes narrowed as she took in the Valentino. "And Adrienne!" she said. "*What* a dress!" She turned to Mrs. Bleecker. "Of course, it would be more appropriate at a cocktail party, but you really can't expect the nanny to understand such things."

"How true," Mrs. Warner added quickly. "Nannies!"

Mrs. Polk, another cotillion committee woman, was passing by. "Oh, is she any good?" she asked Mrs. Warner as if Adrienne weren't standing right there. "I lost mine."

Suddenly there was a cluster of society moms. "Was she deported?" asked a woman in Gucci. "Mine was. *So* rude."

"No," Mrs. Polk replied. "I literally lost her. We were in Bergdorf's, and she handed Lindsay back to me and disappeared. Lost like an Hermès scarf."

"You allow your nanny at social functions?" one of the socialites asked.

Mrs. Warner blanched slightly, then turned to Adrienne. "What are you doing out here?" she asked.

"Excuse me?" Adrienne asked, surprised by the question. Minutes before the party had started, the COW had demanded Adrienne circulate in case there was anything to be done.

"You should keep Emma occupied," Mrs. Warner instructed, becoming more imperious, obviously putting on a little show for her socialite friends.

"Oh, let her stay out here a little longer," Cameron said sweetly. "There's so much for her to see."

Adrienne glanced sharply at Cameron. *Why would she want me out here?* Then she saw the reason.

Brian was standing in the doorway, shifting his weight foot to foot.

Cameron excused herself politely and joined Brian. She slipped her arm through his and beamed at Adrienne.

"Who is that boy?" Mrs. Polk asked. "I've never seen him at any of the charity functions."

Adrienne could see that Brian was having a different impact on the crowd than Cameron might have hoped. There was a hush, and then quite a bit of soft chatter. All the mothers were trying to place Brian. Which, of course, they couldn't.

To Adrienne, Brian looked totally handsome in his Ralph Lauren suit and Charvet tie, but he didn't look very comfortable, as if the clothes didn't belong to him.

"Oh, he's just Cameron's latest boy toy," Mimi said. "Don't worry, she'll tire of him soon enough.'

Mrs. Warner bristled, then laughed. "Oh, these girls and their slang. He's just the son of a friend who happened to be in town this weekend. Mimi, let's go get you a tea cake." She took Mimi's arm and hustled her away from the group.

Cameron began circulating through the room, with Brian silent at her side.

Did she tell him he wasn't allowed to speak, Adrienne wondered, *or is he feeling horribly tongue-tied?*

As she watched, Brian glanced in her direction. His eyes got wide.

This dress is seriously doing its job. I really need to get Kevyn a thank-you gift. Adrienne crossed the room to Cameron and Brian. "Hi," Adrienne said, smiling warmly at Brian.

"Adrienne," Brian said. "You—wow. You look amazing." He couldn't stop staring at her. She flushed with pleasure.

"Thanks. So do you."

Cameron glared at Adrienne through narrowed eyes. "Don't you have to watch Emma?"

"It's all under control," Adrienne said. "Brian, have you had any of the hors d'oeuvres? I made sure they had your favorites since I thought you might be here."

"Really?" Brian said. "That was thoughtful of you."

Adrienne ducked her head as if she were feeling shy. "Well, you know how much I care about you."

"Brian, let me get you a glass of champagne," Cameron said. "Besides, you don't want to get Adrienne in trouble, since she's crashing the party. The longer she's out here, the more likely she'll get caught."

"Oh, of course. Right," Brian said. "See you, Adrienne."

Adrienne watched Cameron stroll off with Brian. Cam glanced back over her shoulder, and then whispered something to Brian. They both laughed.

Knowing Cam, Adrienne thought, *that joke is on me.*

CHAPTER ELEVEN

will the real Parker please stand up?

Liz rested her elbows on the table in the back of the Warners' kitchen. She had come upstairs to give Adrienne a hand with Emma, who sat across from Liz, her nose buried in a thick book. David giggled with Grumpus as they created a huge traffic jam on the table using several metal race cars. Heather had crawled under the table to avoid the antics of David and Grumpus and Emma's obvious disdain.

"How's it going in here?" Adrienne asked, coming back into the kitchen.

"Shockingly smoothly," Liz said. "So, how's the war going out there?"

Adrienne sighed. "My dress was a hit. I mean, Brian looked at me like I was his favorite dessert. But then . . ." Her voice trailed off.

"But then Cameron snapped her fingers and dessert time was over?"

"Exactly," Adrienne said.

"That sucks," Liz said. She really hoped Adrienne would be able to win back Brian, but she had a feeling the longer Cameron had her claws into him, the harder it would be to pry him away.

"Can you go out and peek and see what they're doing?" Adrienne asked. "Maybe Brian is trying to find me."

"Well . . . I'll take a look, but don't get your hopes up."

Liz peeked out the door. *Darn*. She couldn't see anyone. She slipped out and hoped if anyone spotted her she could just claim she was part of the catering crew.

She stepped into the hallway and ran into Isabelle.

"Oh, hi, Liz," Isabelle said morosely.

"Hi, Isabelle," Liz said. "Something wrong?"

"This party is a disaster," Isabelle moaned. "I got a stain on my dress, and they took the worst picture of me."

"I'm sure your dry cleaner can fix it," Liz said.

"I guess . . . but Parker suggested seltzer."

"What?" *Did she just say Parker?*

"Oh, yeah. He said it's some age-old stain-removal trick." She twisted one of her golden curls around her finger. "Who knew that a guy who looks like *that* could add housekeeping to his many charms."

"Parker is here?" Liz tried to figure out what that

meant. The only explanation she could come up with was that Parker was taking Isabelle to the cotillion, too. Didn't Adrienne say the girls were bringing their cotillion escorts to this tea?

"Sure!" Isabelle smiled. "He's over at the buffet getting seltzer. Isn't he the best?"

"Um, I gotta go, Isabelle," Liz said, suddenly having trouble breathing properly.

"See you in Aspen," Isabelle said.

Liz dodged her way through the crowd—she had to get back to the kitchen before Parker spotted her. She just didn't know how she'd behave if she saw him right now.

"Hey," Adrienne said, grabbing her friend's hand. "What's wrong?"

Liz fought back tears. "Parker is out there with Isabelle."

Adrienne's face flooded with sympathy. "I was so focused on Brian that I never even noticed Parker was here," she said. "I'm so sorry."

"Me too," Liz said. "Listen, can you watch Emma now? I really want to get out of here."

Adrienne nodded. "No prob."

Liz got Heather out from under the table, put David in charge of Grumpus, and left through the service entrance.

What is the deal? she wondered. *Who is the real Parker? The sweet guy who treats me like a princess? Or the bad boy dating the rich—and slumming with the help?*

On Sunday, Liz dragged her suitcase to 841 Fifth Avenue. She, the kids, and Dr. M-C were flying first class on an afternoon flight from LaGuardia. Liz was exhausted. She had barely slept, having spent the whole night after the tea worrying about Parker.

At least I'll be able to get some decent sleep in first class, she thought, stepping into the apartment.

"Liz, make Heather quit hitting Grumpus!" David shrieked, racing through the hall after Heather, who ran screaming from him.

"I didn't touch ANYONE!" she yelled. "Because there is NOBODY THERE!"

"Hey!" Liz snapped. "Hey, hey, *HEY*!" She grabbed both kids and yanked them to a stop.

"What about—" David began.

"Grumpus, you too!" Liz ordered. "PLEASE stop!"

David and Heather pouted and glared at each other, but at least they were quiet.

Liz looked around. "Where are your bags?" she asked.

"Mommy said you would pack them," Heather offered.

"We started," David said.

Liz sighed. At least they had started.

They walked into Heather's room. "See?" the little girl said proudly, gesturing to the bed. A huge suitcase sat open on Heather's bed, completely stuffed with toys.

"Uh, I don't think that's exactly what you'll need in Aspen," Liz said. *If this is what Heather packed, what does David have stashed in his suitcase?*

She dashed into David's room, suddenly aware of the time. David scurried around in front of her and stood in front of his bed. "Please don't tell?" he begged.

"Let me see what you packed," Liz said.

"Okay," he said in a small voice.

He stepped aside. On his bed were two suitcases—both empty except for large plastic bags of candy corn he must have been hoarding since Halloween.

"Okay," Liz said, mustering all of the calm force that she could. "We have one hour. Only one hour to pack everything you need."

Soon, Liz had the kids gathering clothes, toys, and equipment for skating. *Thank God I don't have to deal with skis,* she thought.

"Now pack Grumpus!" David ordered. He handed her an empty suitcase.

"David, I really don't think—"

David plopped onto the floor, his face twisted with a barely contained sob.

"Okay, okay, okay," Liz said. "I'll pack for Grumpus as long as you finish your own packing. And," she added, seeing him reach for the bags of candy, "only the things we have already agreed on."

As they were finishing up, Dr. M-C walked in. "Everything ready?" she asked, shuffling through papers in her purse. "The car is downstairs."

"All set. Even Grumpus," Liz said.

Dr. M-C beamed. "Excellent!"

"Do we have a ticket for Grumpus?" David asked. "Do we, Mommy? Do we?"

For a moment, Dr. M-C looked startled, but then she quickly recovered. "Ah, David," she said, "of course we do! One first class ticket for you, one for me, one for Heather"—she reached into her purse and pulled out an invisible ticket—"and one for Grumpus."

David frowned. "That's not a ticket," he said. "That's not really there."

"Well, then, David," Liz said, "if we can't see the ticket, that means it's not there. And if we can't see Grumpus, what does *that* mean?"

"It means Mommy has to look harder!" Dr. M-C said forcefully, shooting Liz a warning look. She reached back into her purse and pulled out a real ticket this time. She handed it to David. "For Grumpus."

"Thanks, Mommy!" David cheered.

Liz gulped. That was obviously *her* ticket. *Am I* not *going now?*

"Kids, go get the elevator!" Dr. M-C said. "Liz will get your bags."

As the children shuffled off, Liz turned to Dr. M-C, her mouth open.

Dr. M-C looked extremely miffed. "Don't worry, Elizabeth. I'll call my travel agent. We'll get you something else. But I don't know why you did that. I'm very disappointed."

"Did what?" Liz asked.

"Try to get David to admit that Grumpus is imaginary. And just when we're about to get started. If he gives up Grumpus now, I'll have no book."

"Sorry, Dr. Markham-Collins," Liz said.

"Now go help the children while I get your ticket arranged."

"Right," Liz said.

She bustled the kids and their luggage downstairs and helped the doormen load the car. Dr. M-C came down, and she and the kids climbed into the town car.

"Well, we're all set!" Dr. M-C said, slipping an e-ticket printed from the computer into Liz's hand.

Liz glanced at the ticket. *Oh joy,* she thought. *I've been bumped down to coach by an invisible kid. And smack into a middle seat.*

"This is going to be a loooooooong flight," she muttered.

CHAPTER TWELVE

putting the plan
in motion

"Adriana," Mrs. Warner called from her bedroom. "Can you get my jewelry case?"

Adrienne sighed and looked around the large entrance hall of the Warner apartment. Piles of suitcases and boxes lined the walls, containing the things that the Warner family regarded as essential on a trip to Saint Moritz, the exclusive Swiss ski resort.

She picked up the heavy case and moved slowly, trying to support the case's awkward shape against her body. She placed it on the dressing table with a thud.

It startled Mrs. Warner, who frowned at her. "Really, Adriana," she muttered. Then she swiveled in her chair to face Adrienne squarely. "I didn't actually need that case," she confided. "I wanted to talk to you alone."

"Oh?" Adrienne said.

"I have to say I was rather disappointed to see that boy Byron at the tea," Mrs. Warner said. "I had hoped you would have accomplished our little goal before then."

"I know, Mrs. Warner," Adrienne replied, "but the tea took up so much time. . . ." Though she *was* pretty pleased by the impact her dress had made on Brian at the tea party.

"Darling, I know!" said Mrs. Warner, turning to her reflection in the mirror and patting the skin under her eyes gently. "I'm exhausted just thinking of all the work I did."

"Uh, right," Adrienne continued. "It's just that I haven't had a chance to spend any time with Brian."

"Well, this vacation should change that," Mrs. Warner said decisively. "While we are away, you have nothing to do but make certain that you get him out of the picture. I managed the Byron problem very deftly at the tea, but as long as he is skulking around Cameron, Mrs. Bleecker and Mrs. Van Tassel will make certain that she is passed over for Deb of the Year."

"I see," Adrienne said.

"Luckily the tea had the desired effect of keeping myself in their good graces," Mrs. Warner added. "But with Cameron . . ."

"Don't worry," Adrienne said. "Now that we're on break I'm sure I'll be able to bring us back together."

"So, we're all set, then." Mrs. Warner stood up and glanced at her pink gold and diamond watch. "Would you be a dear and make certain that everyone is ready?"

Adrienne nodded and left the dressing room. As she entered the hall, she saw Tania giving instructions to the porters who were gathering up the bags.

"For Miss Cameron, this is to be on the boards!" she said, racing up to one of the young men and handing him a pink leather Prada bag.

"What?" he asked.

"On board the jet," Adrienne explained.

"Is what I say. On the boards." Tania shoved the man toward the door. "Go, go, go!"

Emma wandered out of her room, reading an oversized book.

"Light reading for the plane?" Adrienne asked.

"It's a book, a work, a tome, a volume . . . ," Emma began.

"Thesaurus, right?"

"Correct, right, accurate, exact, truthful . . . ," Emma said, leafing through the huge book. "Bye, Adrienne. See you in a week." Emma left, dragging a Prada backpack stuffed full of huge dictionaries and thesauruses.

I wish the au pair at the resort good luck taking care of Emma, Adrienne thought.

Cameron strutted out of her room, wearing a skintight Gucci après-ski outfit. "Oh, hi, Adrienne," she said. She smiled and cocked her head. "Be a dear and take care of

Brian for me while I'm away? He'll be so lonely." Her smile turned into a sneer. "And I know I can trust him with someone like *you*."

She scooped up her dog, Bisquit, who whimpered and shook by the door, terrified by all the commotion. "Ciao," she chirped, and headed for the elevator.

Oh, I'll take care of Brian, all right, Adrienne thought, watching the elevator doors close on the sickening sight of Cameron's smug face. *Don't you worry.*

"What in the devil do you mean that Debi is coming with us?" Mr. Warner bellowed behind Adrienne. She turned and saw Mrs. Warner wringing her hands as Mr. Warner blustered down the hall. Debi LaDeux stood beside Mrs. Warner, imperious as ever.

"But Cameron *has* to keep practicing," Mrs. Warner insisted. "Without Debi, she'll fall behind. She made it through the debutante tea, but she'll never survive the ball without constant supervision."

"Well, as long as Cameron's complaining doesn't ruin this vacation, I suppose it's all right," Mr. Warner said.

"You won't regret it, suh," Debi drawled.

"With what you're charging, I already do," Mr. Warner grumbled.

"Darling!" Mrs. Warner exclaimed.

Debi behaved as if she didn't hear him. "Ah'll just head on downstairs." She left the apartment.

"Where is everybody?" Mr. Warner demanded.

"Why, I think ... well ..." Mrs. Warner glanced around and spotted Adrienne. "Yes, Adriana, where IS everybody?"

"Emma and Cameron are already downstairs," Adrienne said.

"And I'm right here," Graydon said, wandering into the hallway. "What's up?"

"We're trying to leave," Mr. Warner said. "Now can we please get out of here!"

"Sure, Dad," Graydon said. "Don't have a stroke."

Mr. Warner strode out of the apartment, Graydon trailing behind him. As Graydon passed Adrienne he moved closer and whispered, "I'll keep myself warm thinking about you. . . ." He tried to brush her ear with his lips, but Adrienne backed away quickly.

And I'll *try to keep from throwing up,* Adrienne thought.

Graydon winked and followed his dad into the elevator.

"So, we're off," Mrs. Warner said to Adrienne. "I left a Christmas gift for you in the kitchen. Thank you for taking care of the plants while we're gone," she added. "As you know, no one will be here. Bye, Adriana. Happy Christmas—and remember our plans!"

I wonder what my present is, Adrienne thought after Mrs. Warner left. She walked into the kitchen, where a pretty phalenopsis orchid sat with a large card tied to its velvet bow. Pretty, but useless. An envelope sat propped up against the terra-cotta planter.

She slipped open the envelope. It was *full* of cash! There was also a note from Mrs. Warner on her thick gray stationery: *You and Byron make such a cute couple! COW*

Adrienne stretched out on the sofa. *A Fifth Avenue apartment all to myself, a Warner-free break, an envelope full of hundreds, and Cameron's permission to keep Brian from feeling lonely while she's away. It finally feels like Christmas!*

Adrienne grinned. Cameron meant her comment as a put-down. Well, she was going to live to regret tossing out those words at Adrienne so carelessly.

Before she lost her nerve, Adrienne pulled out her cell and hit Brian's speed-dial number. As soon as she heard the phone ring on the other end, her stomach clenched. How was Brian going to respond if she asked him out? He'd turned her down twice already. *Am I crazy?*

She was about to click her phone shut when a woman's voice answered. Brian's mom.

"Hello?" Mrs. Grady said.

Adrienne bit her lip. *Will Mrs. Grady think I'm a total loser for calling Brian after he dumped me?* She cleared her throat and put on a cheery voice. "Hi there, Mrs. Grady, it's Adrienne Lewis."

"Adrienne!" Mrs. Grady said warmly. Adrienne let out the breath she hadn't even realized she was holding. "We haven't seen you for a while. How have you been?"

"Okay," Adrienne said. "Well, I guess you know that Brian and I aren't really seeing each other these days."

"I'm sorry, honey," Mrs. Grady replied. "I had guessed something like that had happened when he began talking about this Cameron person, and you stopped coming over for dinner. Are you all right?"

"I'm fine," Adrienne assured her, not wanting to come across as pathetic. "Is Brian around?"

"No," Mrs. Grady said. "Cameron got him an internship at Wrecker Records over the holidays. That's where he is now."

"Thanks, Mrs. Grady," Adrienne said. "I'll give him a call over there."

"All right, Adrienne," she said. She paused, and then added, "You know, Adrienne, I probably shouldn't say this, because you kids have to make your own decisions, but I hope you can patch things up."

"Me too, Mrs. Grady," said Adrienne. "Me too."

"Wrecker," an operator answered. "How may I help you?"

"I'm looking for an intern named Brian Grady?" Adrienne said.

"One moment please." Hip-hop music blared as the operator put Adrienne on hold.

"Devlin Media Corp Human Resources," a busy female voice said.

"I'm trying to reach Brian Grady," Adrienne said. "He's an intern at Wrecker?"

"It is not company policy to connect people with interns. They aren't supposed to take personal calls."

"Well, it's really important that I speak with him," Adrienne said.

"As I said, it's not our policy. I can't help you."

Adrienne started to panic. *I only have limited time to win Brian back from Cameron—I have to get started NOW!*

She caught a glimpse of herself surrounded by the Warners' opulent furniture. "Listen," she said, in her most adult voice, "I suggest that you connect me with Brian immediately."

"And why, may I ask?" the woman asked, obviously irritated.

"Because my name is Adrienne Lewis, I am calling from Christine Warner's office, and I am a personal friend of Mr. Parker Devlin," Adrienne said.

Silence.

"Uh, I'll put you right through, Ms. Lewis," said the voice, now terrified.

"Thank you," Adrienne said with satisfaction.

A moment later, Brian got on the line.

"Hey, Bri," said Adrienne. "It's me. I didn't get to talk

to you much at the tea. How are you?"

"Uh, I'm cool, Adrienne. What's up? How'd you find me here?"

"Your mom."

"Oh," Brian said.

Well, this is awkward, Adrienne thought. *How do I make this more normal?*

"Listen, do you want to go grab a coffee?" she blurted. "The Warners are off to Aspen, Liz is on her way to Aspen, Tamara and Lily are both busy, even Tania and Kane are gone, and I'm bored out of my mind."

Brian laughed. "Actually, you sound pretty caffeinated already."

Adrienne laughed too. "Okay, maybe I should have some nice green tea."

"Nah, you never were one for the organic stuff."

"You either," Adrienne pointed out, encouraged that he hadn't found an excuse to get off the phone. "At least *I'm* not afraid of tofu."

"Hey! Food shouldn't jiggle," Brian protested. "It's just wrong."

"So what do you say?" she pressed. "We'll go to a tofu-free zone."

Brian paused, and Adrienne crossed her fingers.

"Sure, why not," he said. "How about Starbucks at Fifty-Seventh and Lex, around six?"

"Perfect. See you then." Adrienne clicked off. "Yes!" she shrieked, jumping into the air. Then she glanced at the clock. She had forty minutes to change into something of Cameron's and meet Brian.

"You have got to be kidding me!" Adrienne giggled. "The lead singer of Stud can only work if he brings his teddy bear?"

Brian nodded. "Someone put it in the lost-and-found and he totally freaked."

"I don't know, Bri, you are seriously messing with my worldview," Adrienne said, grinning over her second mocha eggnog latte.

"You always said Stud was a bunch of posers anyway," Brian reminded her. "You could say I'm strengthening your argument."

"Hmm. Good point," Adrienne said. She took a sip of her coffee drink. The peaks of foam tickled her nose.

Brian grinned at her.

"What?" she asked.

He reached forward. "The foam. You look like you have snow on your nose." He dabbed her nose with a napkin.

Adrienne shut her eyes, barely able to contain her glee. *This is such a boyfriend thing for him to do.*

Her eyes flicked open again. "Thanks," she said.

"Yeah ...," he said. His voice trailed off as he studied her face.

She suddenly grew self-conscious. *Is he comparing me with Cameron? I hope he doesn't recognize this outfit.*

After a brief awkward moment, Brian and Adrienne quickly found themselves chatting away as if there was no tension between them at all. Brian even ignored the beeps of his cell phone. Adrienne carefully avoided any mention of Cameron, and Brian did the same.

"It seems like you really love being at Wrecker," she said.

"It's awesome," Brian said. "And it's not just meeting all these rockers. It's cool watching how a song comes together. The way things get manipulated in the studio."

"Do you want to learn to engineer?" Adrienne asked.

Brian shrugged. "Maybe," he said. He wrapped his hands around his mug and glanced at his watch. "Wow, is that the time?" he said. "We've been talking for two hours!"

"No wonder I'm hungry," Adrienne said, hoping he'd get the hint.

He gazed into her eyes again. "I forgot how easy it is to talk to you," he said. "Cam just isn't all that interested in stuff like—" He cut himself off and stared down at his coffee mug.

I'm not going to let Cam screw this up for me. Especially

since she isn't even here, Adrienne thought. "It's okay," she said. "You can say her name."

Brian nodded and ran his hand through his dark hair. "Right," he said, a slight flush rising in his cheeks. "But I don't want to talk about her right now."

"Fine by me," Adrienne said.

"So, you want to grab some dinner?" he asked.

It's working! "Sure," she said. "I'll call my parents." She reached into her bag and felt around. "Oh, no! I left my cell on the kitchen table at the Warners'. I need to go back and get it."

"Okay," Brian said. "I'll call my mom and let her know. Then we can stop by the Warners', grab your phone, and figure out where to eat."

Or maybe we can just order in . . . , Adrienne thought.

———————————

Adrienne and Brian were settled on the sofa in the kitchen, the fireplace blazing. They had ordered in Japanese food, which they paired with a bottle of Chardonnay that Adrienne pulled from the extensive wine collection. Now they were deciding what movie to watch on the huge flat-screen TV.

Adrienne moved her toes toward Brian at the other end of the sofa and wiggled them under his thigh for warmth.

"Are you cold?" he asked, taking an Hermès lap blanket from the arm of the sofa and throwing it over her legs. As he reached forward to tuck it in under her, Adrienne sat up, and they found themselves face-to-face.

"It's weird being with you like this," he said softly. "It's like everything's back the way it was."

"I-I know what you mean," Adrienne said. She held her breath, willing him to kiss her.

He did.

Brian's lips pressed hard against Adrienne's as he pulled her close. She ran her hands up his back and clung to him, letting herself feel comforted by his kisses, letting them wash away all of the hurt and fear and anger she had been feeling.

I can't believe it, Adrienne thought. *This is amazing. He's mine again!*

"Adriana!" a voice said as the overhead lights in the kitchen snapped on. "Are you in here?"

"Mr. and Mrs. Warner!" Adrienne exclaimed.

Brian and Adrienne instantly separated as if they were magnets repelling. Somehow Brian was at the window and Adrienne was perched at the table. *I think we just broke all the laws of physics,* she thought.

Mr. and Mrs. Warner walked into the kitchen. Mr. Warner immediately went to the liquor cabinet and poured himself a scotch.

"What are you doing home?" Adrienne asked.

"No snow," Mr. Warner said. "We got to the airport,

and our pilot told us it was like July in Saint Moritz. I called the resort and offered to buy them a snow machine, but they wouldn't do it." He downed his drink and poured another. He turned and faced them. "But the real question is, what the hell are you two doing here?"

Mrs. Warner gave Adrienne a small smile, then touched her husband's arm. "Oh darling, I thought I told you that I had asked Adriana to check on things while we were gone."

"Ah." Mr. Warner began rummaging through the huge refrigerator.

"Hey!" Cameron said, walking into the kitchen. "Bri! You got my message! Great! I *knew* you'd be here."

Brian looked confused, then went blank. "Uh, yeah, sure," he mumbled. He stared at his sneakers.

"Cool! Let's go out." She grabbed Brian's hand.

As Cameron dragged Brian past Adrienne, he said, "So, uhm, see you around, Adrienne."

Adrienne's mouth dropped open and tears stung her eyes. *How can he diss me like this after the time we just spent together?* Adrienne shook her head. *Cameron has him completely whipped.*

"I am *so* happy you are here, Adrienne," Mrs. Warner said, completely ignoring the stricken look on Adrienne's face. "Mr. Warner and I are just here to drop off the children. We're leaving for Palm Beach, just the two of us."

"Can't wait," Mr. Warner said, dumping a pile of meats, cheeses, and pâté onto the counter.

"I know, darling, I know," she said, smiling. "So, Adriana, we really need you to step up to the plate. We'll make it worth your time."

Luckily, Emma came in, giving Adrienne another moment to compose herself.

"Salutations, greetings, acknowledgments, hello, Adrienne," Emma said, dropping her bag on the floor.

"So, as I was saying, would you be a dear and stay here with Emma? Tania will be returning as well to handle the nights. Wonderful. All right, darling, let's go!"

Mr. Warner picked up his platter of snacks and tucked the bottle of scotch under his arm. Mrs. Warner followed him, regaling him with all the friends they'll be THRILLED to see once they got to Palm Beach.

A moment later, Adrienne and Emma were left alone in the quiet kitchen.

"Looks like it's just you and me," Emma said.

"It always is," Adrienne replied.

CHAPTER THIRTEEN

out of the closet

Arriving late at Dr. M–C's house in Aspen, Liz didn't really notice much about it except that it was large, dark, and somewhere in the woods just outside of Aspen. Fighting a slight headache from the thin mountain air, Liz helped the sleepy kids (two real, one imaginary) into their bedrooms, called her mother to let her know she had arrived safely, and then followed Dr. M–C down the hall to the room where she was to sleep.

"This is it," Dr. M–C announced, opening the door to the tiny bedroom. "It used to be a broom closet," she added, gesturing toward the brooms hanging on the back of the door. "Your bath is down the hall. See you in the morning."

Liz said good night, changed out of her clothes, fell into the bed, and was sound asleep in no time.

The next morning, the light passing across her face woke her, and Liz sat up and looked around. "This is the fanciest broom closet I've ever seen," she murmured.

The room was tiny, but the walls were paneled in a rough-hewn cedar wood and smelled wonderful. Slender windows looked out onto a snow-covered garden next to the garage, and the light streamed in through a glass door that opened onto a tiny terrace.

Liz hopped out of bed and rose to investigate, pulling her comforter around her shoulders. She opened the door, and a burst of cold air blew through the room. Liz stepped outside, her bare feet tingling on the snowy wood deck.

I have never been anywhere so beautiful, Liz thought, looking out over the valleys and mountains that spread out at her feet like a carpet. The land fell away from the wooden terraces of Dr. M-C's amazing house, giving Liz the impression that she was flying over the snowy landscape.

The pristine sight banished all of Liz's resentment over being stuck in coach so that Grumpus could fly first class.

Liz began to shiver, so she stepped back into the house, rubbing her shoulders against the crisp, thin air. She closed the door to the terrace and bundled back up in her cozy bed. She glanced at the clock on the wall. It was early; the time difference from New York meant that she was up two hours earlier than normal.

I wonder what time I'm expected to start taking care of the kids? Liz thought. She had never gone on vacation with Dr.

M–C before. *Am I working 24/7 while I'm here?*

After a long, hot shower, Liz changed into a pretty pale blue turtleneck sweater and a pair of jeans, and debated wearing the pale blue Ugg boots she had bought for the trip. Were Uggs over? Would she look like an idiot? A poser? A draft blew through the room, and Liz decided she would wear them—it was too cold not to.

Liz walked down the long hall and stepped through a pair of glass doors into an incredible room. It was huge, divided into three large sections by timber-framed white plaster walls. Windows stretched floor to ceiling, and a series of flying staircases led to the bedrooms upstairs. The room had an unfinished, rural feel, with hand-hewn beams and wide plank floors. Everywhere she looked, light streamed in through the paned windows, washing over the comfortable leather furniture and enormous patterned carpets. Liz stared at the cathedral ceilings and admired a long balcony that hung over the living room, giving the third floor the same view as the second.

In the middle of the room, a large pit contained a roaring fire, the flue hanging over it like a hat.

"Ain't much in the way of crackling," said a voice just outside her view. "But it throws off enough heat."

Startled, Liz walked farther into the room. A pleasant-looking older woman with short white hair stood wiping a glass clean with a cloth in her hand.

"Billie Baird," the woman said with a smile. "Are you Miss Braun?"

"Yes," Liz said. "But please call me Liz."

"And you call me Billie," the woman said. "A package came for you. I put it on the table."

"Great, thanks."

Billie vanished through a swinging door into what Liz guessed was the kitchen. Liz looked around and spotted a box sitting on a low, Italian-tiled coffee table.

It's so much homier here than back at Dr. M-C's Fifth Avenue apartment, Liz thought as she crossed the room. *Clearly someone else did the decorating!*

Liz knelt down beside the table and opened the slim, velvet-covered box. Her dark eyes widened as she pulled out a thick platinum charm bracelet. She gasped when she saw the small diamond snowflake charm dangling from the chain.

"'Welcome to Aspen. —Parker'" she read aloud from the card. She held up the bracelet and let the light dance off its shining surfaces. *Maybe the whole thing with Isabelle is a big fat nothing*, Liz thought.

"Elizabeth!" Dr. M-C appeared at the top of the stairs flanked by Heather and David. "We have a schedule to keep!"

"We do?" Liz said, slipping the bracelet back into the box. "We just got here."

"Precisely. Time's wasting. I have to get to work. I have the children's itinerary right here." She held up a clipboard. "Their ski lesson starts in just a few minutes."

"Have you guys skied before?" Liz asked.

Heather nodded. "I fell down a lot," she said. She didn't look too thrilled to be making another attempt.

"Grumpus doesn't need lessons," David said. "He's an expert!"

"Oh, David, that's wonderful," Dr. M-C gushed. "He can help Heather with her form."

Heather rolled her eyes.

"Grumpus knows you don't like him," David said. "He doesn't like you, either."

"I don't care," Heather declared.

David giggled. "Grumpus just stuck his tongue out at you!"

"David," Liz said in a warning tone. He made a face, but stopped teasing Heather.

"We want to see some improvement by the time we leave," Dr. M-C. said. "That's why I've hired someone training for the Olympic team to be your instructor. He'll be here soon. We can't keep Lars waiting!"

"Well, then, let's get you into your ski clothes and grab your equipment," Liz said, heading for the wide stairs.

She joined them at the landing. Dr. M-C handed Liz the clipboard, then vanished back into her room. As Liz followed the kids down the hall, she scanned the itinerary.

Her mouth dropped open. *Wow. Dr. M-C has scheduled these kids within an inch of their lives!* Ski lessons. Skating. More ski lessons. Several events at the opera house. *And I'll also have those note sessions with Dr. M-C,* Liz realized. *When am I ever going to get a chance to see Parker?*

"Do I have to go?" Heather whined when Liz stepped into her room.

"Don't you like to ski?" Liz asked.

"It's cold and it's wet and the ski boots are too heavy," Heather complained.

"Well, maybe with some lessons with Lars you'll start having more fun," Liz said.

"Maybe . . ." Heather didn't sound very convinced.

"Give it a try," Liz said. "If you really, *really* hate it, maybe we can come up with another activity that your mom will approve of."

Heather sighed, but she turned and began pulling ski clothes from her dresser.

One down, one to go, Liz thought, going to David's room. *Make that two more,* she reminded herself. *Grumpus will undoubtedly be joining us on the slopes.*

"David, how are you doing?" Liz asked, going into his room.

"Grumpus needs help," David said.

"I think you need some help, too," Liz said. She knelt

down and rebuttoned and rezipped everything David was wearing.

"Now get Grumpus ready," David insisted. "He needs his skis!"

"Well, get them for him," Liz said. It was bad enough catering to the whims of little kids and a crazed psychologist. She wasn't going to wait on an imaginary child, too! At least not when Dr. M-C wasn't around.

David reluctantly mimed handing skis to Grumpus, and Liz went into her room to get herself ready.

Liz had skied all of once before, on a Pheasant-Berkeley school trip. She had done well for a beginner, but had never ventured beyond the easiest of trails. *Hmm. Maybe I can get Lars to give me a few tips, too.*

She stepped into the hall. "Everybody ready?" she called.

"Liz," Heather whined, appearing in the doorway of her room. "I'm hot."

Liz stifled a laugh. In her snowsuit and multiple layers, Heather looked more like the Michelin tire man than a child.

"We'll be outdoors in a minute, and then you'll be fine," Liz said.

David stepped into the hall and frowned. "I have to go to the bathroom," he said.

Liz sighed. *Back to square one.*

Finally they were ready. By the time they got downstairs, Lars, a tall, blond, college-age guy, was standing just outside the sliding doors of the living room. He wasn't particularly handsome, but he had a sweet, wholesome face. Dr. M-C was going over her goals for the children with him.

"Oh, there you are," Dr. M-C said, a trace of irritation in her voice. "We were beginning to wonder what happened to you."

"Grumpus needed some special attention," Liz said. *If David can use Grumpus to his advantage*, Liz figured, *so can I.*

"Grumpus, yes, of course." Dr. M-C smiled broadly. "Do you have your notebook?"

Liz nodded. She had stashed the notebook in her fanny pack, along with a few contraband snacks to use as bribes if the kids started acting up.

"Good," Dr. M-C said. "Now I want you to keep very careful notes on everything Grumpus does. We'll review your observations at the end of every day."

Oh, joy, Liz thought.

"Liz, where are your skis?" Dr. M-C demanded. "We don't want to waste any more of Lars's time."

"I don't own skis," Liz said. "I thought we'd have time to rent them."

"I'll bring a pair for you tomorrow," Lars promised in a light Nordic accent. "For today, you will be there to help with the children. That will be most important."

"Thanks," Liz said. She could tell he had jumped in to prevent a problem with Dr. M-C. Obviously, the good doctor had already proven to Lars what a demanding nut-job she was.

"My pleasure," Lars said. He smiled, revealing dimples.

Together, Liz and Lars managed to get Heather and David into their skis and out the door. Dr. M-C owned a house right on Buttermilk, the slope famous in Aspen for being kind to beginners. All they had to do was ski out the sliding doors and they were already on the mountain. No need for lift tickets, lift lines, or, Liz realized, pesky tourists on a budget.

"Snow!" David cried. He used his ski poles to kick up snow. "Look, it's snowing!"

"Not funny," Heather said.

"You should slide the skis, Heather," Lars instructed. "You don't need to pick them up as if you were walking."

Heather tried to do as Lars said, but her front leg slid so far in front of her that she was trapped in a split.

"Help!" she shrieked. "My legs are going to rip off!"

Liz shook her head and helped Heather back up to a normal stance. She glanced at Lars and saw that he was trying to get David to stop making snow angels and not get smacked by the little boy's skis.

"David, get up," Liz ordered, holding Heather upright by clutching her under the armpits.

"Oh, okay." David reluctantly got back up to his feet, as Lars shot Liz a thankful look.

10:13 *Grumpus won 27 gold medals for skiing and snowboarding and never once did he have to wear a hat, so David wants to know why HE has to wear one.*

10:15 *Grumpus thinks it's hilarious when David falls down. So David falls down a lot "just to make Grumpus laugh."*

10:22 *Grumpus objects to Heather having a turn with Lars.*

Liz was bored out of her mind. The kids were behaving better now that Lars had really begun the lesson. So Liz started taking notes for Dr. M-C to keep from noticing how cold she was.

It's because I'm just standing here, Liz realized, stamping her feet. *I'd be a lot warmer if I were actually skiing!*

10:47 *Grumpus has been strangely silent—perhaps he has skied away?*

10:50–11:05 *Ignore previous note. Grumpus has been making nonstop demands for the last fifteen minutes.*

"Maybe it's time for a break," Liz suggested. She could

tell the kids were reaching their limit. Heather was shivering, and David had plopped down in the snow and didn't seem interested in getting up.

"Grumpus wants hot chocolate," David announced.

"If Grumpus gets hot chocolate, I do too!" Heather shouted.

"Is there a place nearby where we can we get them something hot to drink?" Liz asked Lars.

"Sure!" Lars said. "There's a lodge at the bottom of the hill. I can drive you all down."

"Great," Liz said. "Why don't we call it quits and grab some?"

"Sounds good to me," Lars said.

"Liz!" a voice called behind her.

Liz's heart fluttered at the sound of Parker's voice. She turned as he skied up to her in a spray of snow. He looked devastatingly hot in his ski gear, his silver Ray-Bans, and perfect form.

"Hi," Liz said, grateful that the first time Parker saw her in Aspen she wasn't bumbling around like a newbie on a pair of rented skis. "I got your gift. It's beautiful. I meant to call to thank you, but—"

"Liz, it's time for hot chocolate!" Heather complained. "I'm freezing."

"One sec," Liz said, focusing on Parker.

"Grumpus thinks you aren't paying enough attention,"

David scolded. He stumbled forward a few feet on his skis, Lars gliding alongside him.

Liz glanced sheepishly at Parker. "I think Grumpus may be right. You are *much* too distracting."

"I'm glad to hear it." Parker grinned mischievously. "So when can we get together?"

"I'm not really sure," Liz admitted. "Dr. M–C has all these plans . . ."

"Well, give me a call once you know," Parker said. "I'm heading up to the Highlands now."

"Those are serious slopes," Lars said.

"Know 'em like the back of my hand," Parker said. "My friends and I have been hanging up there even before they got hot."

Friends like Isabelle? Liz wondered.

"Have fun with the rest of the bunnies," Parker said. He gave Liz a quick kiss. "And don't fall for the ski instructor," he whispered. "It's so cliché."

Liz giggled. "Don't worry," she promised. "I'm nothing if not unique."

Parker leaned back on his skis, a slow smile spreading across his face. "You got that right."

Then he turned and skied away, a gorgeous sight in the already gorgeous landscape.

CHAPTER FOURTEEN

you should see
the place in Vienna

*M*om *had nothing to worry about,* Liz thought four days later as she soaked in the hot tub in the enclosed patio just off Dr. M–C's Aspen living room. *I am definitely here to work!*

Every muscle hurt from learning to ski, falling, and grabbing kids. She'd been kept so busy by David and Heather during the day, and then by Dr. M–C's demands to help her work on the book at night, that Liz had barely seen Parker other than in passing.

But tonight! *Tonight is going to be awesome,* she thought, *and all thanks to Parker's smooth moves.* Parker had dropped by (after daily flirty phone calls and text messages) and had persuaded Dr. M–C to let Liz go out with him. Although Dr. M–C had been reluctant to lose Liz's secretarial skills, she relented—once Parker invited the doc and her kids to his parents' ultra-exclusive Christmas party.

Liz climbed out of the hot tub, wrapped herself in the luxurious robe that had been provided in her tiny broom closet/bedroom, and headed upstairs to dress.

She frowned as she looked in her suitcase. *Parker never told me what we're doing,* Liz realized, *so I have no idea what I should wear. And even if I DID know, would I have the right outfit?*

For the last four days Liz had been checking out what the other girls in Aspen were wearing. She fit right in on Buttermilk, where the little kids, the older couples, and the beginners tended to ski. But the few times she'd spotted Parker in the Lodge, or in town, the girls in his orbit wore Chanel, Prada, and the high-priced Moon Boots that J.Lo was recently photographed in.

Liz sighed. She didn't have a lot of clothing options. All she could do was find a sweater that flattered her complexion and tight velvet jeans that highlighted her long legs and hope for the best.

"Parker, come in," Dr. M-C's voice boomed up the stairs.

Uh-oh. I'd better get down there and rescue him, Liz thought. She applied a fresh coat of lip gloss and hurried downstairs.

Parker smiled when he saw her. She felt her knees go weak. *I'm glad we decided not to go skiing together,* she thought. *I'd fall right over.* There was just something about Parker that hit her hard every time she saw him. She noticed with relief that he was wearing a sweater and cords—nothing over-the-top.

"So what do you two have planned?" Dr. M-C asked.

Parker slipped his hand around her waist, his fingertips brushing against her skin, and Liz felt herself tingle.

"Liz hasn't had a chance to see much of the town," Parker said. "So I thought we'd check out some shops, and then swing by a friend's party. Don't worry," he added, "I'll get Liz back at a completely reasonable hour. I know how important taking care of David and Heather is to her."

Dr. M-C beamed. "Have a wonderful time, Liz. I know you're in the best of hands. And Parker," she said as she walked them to the door, "do give my best to your parents. I am *so* looking forward to their Christmas party."

Once outside, Parker opened the door of his gleaming Range Rover, and Liz slipped inside. Parker dashed around the car, then got in behind the wheel. He swiveled to face her.

"So hi," he said, brushing a strand of her dark hair out of her face.

"Hi," she replied.

"I was beginning to think I'd never get a chance to be alone with you," he said. He tipped her face up and kissed her softly.

Liz kissed him back, thrilled to be this close to him again. *It* has *been a long time*, she thought as she finally pulled away to smile at him.

He grinned back. "Now, *that's* the Liz I remember." He started up the car, and they drove into Aspen.

"It looks like a town from some Western movie," Liz observed, checking out the small wooden and brick buildings.

"Well, it did start out as a mining camp, and there's a whole historic preservation movement happening here," Parker explained, taking Liz's hand and helping her out of the car. "But somehow I doubt Cartier had a shop catering to the miners!"

Liz laughed. Parker was right. Aspen was a weird cross between cowboy-ville and Madison Avenue. Limos fought for parking; socialites and movie stars sipped hot cocoa and coffee; store owners rung up thousands of dollars of sales— and all against the stunning backdrop of the mountains and old, rustic buildings.

Despite all the glitz and glamour, though, Parker made Liz feel as if she belonged there—not in Aspen so much as she belonged right by his side.

After showing Liz his favorite shops, Parker pulled up to the gates of Mimi von Fallschirm's Aspen home. As the car rolled along the long stone driveway, Liz realized there wasn't even a hint of snow on the pavement.

"Are they so special they have their own weather?" Liz joked.

Parker laughed. "Mimi would like to think so. But no, it's just a heated driveway. Makes sense up here." They pulled up in front of the door, and a valet took the keys and drove the car away.

"The house is ridiculous," Parker said, shaking his head. "It's so over-the-top." He rang the bell, and a servant opened the door.

Liz's jaw dropped as they stepped inside.

The entry hall was part baronial manor, part Adirondack lodge, with tapestries hanging from the walls, and suits of armor standing sentry every few feet. Two stuffed polar bears reared in the corners, and an enormous chandelier made of hundreds of antlers hung from the ceiling. Animal heads glared down from perches high above them.

Mimi sashayed up to them, her fur-trimmed dress fitted close to her slim body, a Cosmo in her hand. Suddenly Liz felt underdressed.

"Hello, Parker," she said. She kissed him on both cheeks, and tossed her long black hair over her shoulder. "Who's your—" She cut herself off when she recognized Liz. "Well, Liz! Welcome to Aspen! I didn't know your family had a house here!"

"They don't," Liz said. "I'm staying with—"

"Friends of my parents," Parker interjected.

"Oh, really?" Mimi said. "Interesting. I had no idea Liz had become so close to your family."

Liz looked at Parker. *It was nice of him to jump in for me,* she thought, *but why did he need to lie to Mimi? She knows I'm a nanny. Is he ashamed that I'm here working?* For the first time that day, she felt out of place.

"Come," Mimi ordered. "This way."

Liz and Parker stepped through an enormous archway and down into the huge living room. It was filled with dark oil portraits in gilded frames, and heavy, oversized furniture. There was a DJ at one end of the room, where the carpet had been rolled up and kids were dancing. Waiters in red jackets served drinks from silver trays.

"Your house is amazing," Liz said, looking out the windows at the moonlight on the snow.

Mimi shrugged. "You should see the place in Vienna," she replied.

Liz spotted several girls and their dates from Cameron's tea party. The stoned brunette from the movie premiere—Cynthia—was also there, tottering on glittering heels and laughing loudly. It looked as if the party had been going on for some time already.

Parker's cell beeped. He pulled it from his pocket and glanced at the screen. "Oops, gotta take this," he said. He pecked Liz on the cheek and wandered away, a hand over his ear to drown out the party sounds.

Liz watched Parker weave his way through the dancing kids and out of the room, wondering what could be so important that he had to go have a private conversation.

She decided to shrug it off and turned to Mimi. "So, Mimi—"

"Excuse me," Mimi said, moving away from Liz as if she didn't want to be seen with her.

Whoa, Liz thought, as Mimi joined two tall guys doing tequila shots. *Being a princess sure doesn't mean you have any manners.*

Maybe a drink will help. Liz grabbed a glass of champagne off the tray of a passing waiter. Sipping the crisp, bubbling drink, she made her way through the room, hoping to find a familiar, or at least friendly, face.

She leaned against the wall and scanned the crowd. She spotted two P-B girls dancing together, their heads thrown back, their arms up in the air. A few guys bobbed around them.

The dark-haired girl in the micro-mini is Leigh Penbroke, Liz thought. *She's in my English class. The redhead in the suede is . . .* Liz shook her head. She couldn't remember the other girl's name. She decided to go talk to them anyway. Better risk getting the girl's name wrong than look like a total loser hanging by the wall.

Liz downed her champagne and then picked up another glass on her way over to the P-B girls. As she wiggled her way through the dancers, she was relieved to see that many of the girls were dressed as casually as she was.

She sidled up to Leigh and the other P–B girl and began moving in time to the techno drumbeat.

"Leigh!" Liz called over the music.

Leigh's forehead wrinkled as she focused on Liz. "I know you," she said. "You're someone I know."

"Liz Braun," Liz said. "From Pheasant-Berkeley."

"Right!" Leigh said. "From there."

She's totally wasted, Liz realized.

"Miranda," Leigh said to the other girl. "This is Liz. From school."

"I know," Miranda said. "I'm standing right here."

"I didn't know you were a Mimi-ite," Leigh said.

"She's going to be Deb of the Year, you know," Miranda said.

"Which is going to kill Cameron!" Leigh said, giggling.

The music changed to a slow song, and Leigh slung her arm across Liz's shoulders. Liz tried to shrug the girl off, but it didn't work. *Where is Parker?*

"We're not debs," she said in a loud stage whisper.

"But we're SO rich!" Miranda said, laughing hysterically.

"That's why Mimi likes us," Leigh said.

"Why does Mimi like you?" Miranda asked.

The two girls stared at her expectantly. *Great.* She doubted Mimi liked her—or even thought much about her—at all.

"I'm here with Parker Devlin," Liz said. Well, that was true, and it made her feel like at least she'd been invited.

Leigh's eyes widened. "Ohmigod," she said. "Are you—?" She turned and whispered something to Miranda, who giggled.

"Am I what?" Liz demanded.

"Nothing," Leigh said. "It's just, well, we heard that Parker was sometimes hooking up with someone who, well, someone not in his usual crowd."

There's been gossip about me? Liz thought. Then she realized: *Of course there is.*

"Where *is* Parker?" Miranda asked.

"He went to take a phone call," Liz said.

"Well, send him our way," Leigh said with a giggle. "We can always count on him for a good time."

"Ooh, I love this song!" Miranda squealed. She grabbed Leigh's hands and pulled her into a dance groove.

Liz scanned the room and didn't see anyone she felt comfortable approaching. *What is making Parker take so long?* She decided to go look for him.

She ducked into the long hallway Parker had disappeared into. Thick carpeting silenced her footsteps, and she startled a couple making out on a love seat as she passed. More stuffed animal heads stared down at her accusingly. "Hey, don't blame me—I'm practically a vegetarian," she told them.

A loud burst of male laughter floated down the hall. Curious, Liz peered through an archway. Parker sat perched on the back of a leather sofa, talking to a group of guys playing pool. Tables set up with chessboards, checker boards, and cards were scattered throughout the dark room.

"Liz! Come on in," Parker said when he glanced over at the doorway.

Liz stepped into the room. *Was he just hanging out in here the whole time?* "I was wondering what happened to you," she said.

"Oh, yeah, sorry." He reached out for her and wrapped his arms around her waist. The other guys grinned broadly.

Liz held herself slightly away from Parker. She was miffed that he had just abandoned her like that.

Parker didn't seem to notice. He nuzzled her neck, and then took a swig of beer.

"So, I'm Liz," she said to the guys at the pool table, irritated that Parker hadn't bothered to introduce her.

"Oh, sorry," Parker said. "Liz, these are some seriously shady characters, and I advise you to stay clear of them all."

The guys laughed. The tall guy with shaggy blond hair holding a pool cue nodded. "He's right, Liz. We're a bunch of desperados."

"Oh, I don't know," Liz joked, determined not to allow her feelings to show. "I've seen worse."

The blond grinned. "I'm Kyle, that's Jono, and the guy losing the big bucks because he's such a bad player is the always miserable Winston."

"We haven't seen one another since the last time we were in Aspen," Parker explained. "We were just reminiscing about our wayward youth." He looked at Liz and smiled.

His eyes had a funny shine to them. *He's stoned*, Liz realized. *That's probably why he got so easily distracted.*

Liz was bugged that he had gone off and gotten high, but it at least explained why he had just vanished. She didn't get high herself, and Parker knew that. Well, maybe he'll still redeem himself.

As if he could read her mind, he gave her a gentle squeeze. "Sorry I left you alone out there. Was it brutal?"

"Brutally boring," Liz said, deciding to let it slide.

"Hey, Liz," Kyle said. "Wanna hit a few?" He held out the pool cue.

Parker took Liz's hand. "Liz came to a party, not to watch you three losers make fools of yourselves at the table. Besides, she doesn't want to hear our old stories."

"Or maybe you don't want her to hear them," Winston teased. He waggled his reddish eyebrows at Liz. "The things this guy gets up to."

Liz laughed. "Don't I know it."

Parker kissed Liz. "And she still wants me!"

Liz felt as if she had played the game right: She didn't get all prissy and huffy, she didn't let them intimidate her by making her feel excluded, and best of all, Parker was leading her back to the party room.

Parker guided her smoothly onto the dance floor. They began to move in synch, and Liz realized he was a really good, sexy dancer. Moving very close to her but never touching her, Parker seemed to anticipate her every shimmer and step. He put his hands on her hips and pulled her into him, continuing to move to the beat.

"You're a really hot dancer," he whispered.

"You too," Liz said. She flushed with pleasure. She didn't want the music to stop. But she also didn't want to wind up making out with Parker on the dance floor with everyone watching! She pulled herself away.

Parker looked down at her and grinned. "Getting a little too heavy?" he asked. He grabbed her hand and twirled her, then started dancing in an insane, overdramatic way. Liz burst out laughing.

"You mock me?" Parker demanded. He twirled around and then acted as if he were dizzy. He fell onto Liz, who was laughing so hard, she could barely hold him up.

"I think we need to take a break," Liz said, gasping.

"Your wish is my command." Parker said.

Liz and Parker found the bar again. "Water, my good man. Straight up!" Parker ordered from the bartender.

"I think I'll have mine on the rocks," Liz said.

She settled onto a bar stool and surveyed the room again. Parker became startled beside her. "Huh," he said.

"What is it?" Liz asked. She peered at the crowd, wondering what he was reacting to.

Isabelle had just arrived.

"Is there a problem?" Liz asked, her body tense.

"What? No, I'm just surprised to see Isabelle here. I thought she was arriving next week."

His cell phone beeped. Parker glanced at it, then gave Liz a sheepish smile. "I know. I know. But this one is important." He walked back out into the hall.

Well, at least I know it's not Isabelle calling this time, Liz thought as she watched Mimi greet Isabelle. The girls glanced over at Liz and started whispering.

Oh, great, Liz thought. *Way to be subtle, girls.*

Suddenly, Liz didn't feel like being at the party anymore. She was tired of the mysterious phone calls, didn't want to be left stranded again by Parker, and didn't want to have to deal with Isabelle and Mimi.

Please come back now, Parker, Liz pleaded silently. *And get me out of here.*

"Sorry about that," Parker said, coming up behind her.

"You sure get a lot of phone calls," Liz commented. She sounded more whiney than she had wanted.

Parker ran a hand through his dark hair. "Well, yeah,"

he admitted. "It's catching up with everyone. We only see one another a few times a year."

"That's cool," Liz said, sliding off the bar stool. "Listen, it's been great, but I have a really early day tomorrow, so I should go."

"You do?" he said.

"I do," she said, hoping they could take a long, romantic drive home.

"That's too bad," Mimi said, appearing suddenly. "Don't worry about calling a cab, Liz. I have a car and driver to take people home if they can't drive."

"I didn't drive over," Liz explained. "I came with—"

"Why don't you take the car, Liz," Parker interrupted. He waved at a bunch of kids who had just entered the party. "I should stick around and say hi to a few more people. And, like you said, you have to get up early."

"Please," Mimi said. "I'm happy to have you driven home."

I bet you are, Liz thought, noticing Isabelle hovering in the arched bay window.

One of the newcomers to the party came up to Parker and clapped him on the shoulder. "Devlin the Devil!" the guy greeted him. "I thought you'd be here!"

"Walton!" Parker gave the guy an intricate handshake. "Are the rest of the team in town yet?"

Liz stood there as Parker and Walton compared notes

on who was in Aspen and who wasn't. She was acutely aware of Mimi waiting. Isabelle had now moved to the outskirts of the new group of kids, chatting them up. *Homing in on Parker, no doubt,* Liz thought.

"So, I'll ring the driver?" Mimi asked, though Liz knew it wasn't really a question.

"Well, okay," Liz said. "I guess it makes the most sense." She didn't want to make a scene in front of Mimi.

Parker finally pulled his attention from Walton. "Sorry, Liz, but I gotta catch up with the crew! And I don't want you to get in trouble with the doc."

Liz forced a smile onto her face. "Of course."

Hiding her disappointment, Liz left. She stepped into the black car, which bore on its doors the painted crest of Prince Von Fallschirm.

What a royal pain, Liz thought.

And then the tears came.

CHAPTER FIFTEEN

Grumpus calls

The caffeine in Liz's morning coffee was not doing its job. Not after her night of tossing and turning. One question just kept going around and around in her head: *What is going on between Parker and Isabelle?*

Why did he want Liz to go home without him? So that he could stay at the party and, what—flirt with Isabelle? Or maybe do *more* than flirt?

"Grumpus wants to go ice skating!" David shouted, interrupting Liz's gloomy inner monologue.

"Me too!" Heather exclaimed.

"Okay, okay," Liz said. *It will be a lot easier than skiing,* she figured. "Go get your skates, and I'll let your mom know where we're going."

"Yay!" David cheered.

Liz poured herself another cup of coffee as the kids went to get their skates. Her cell rang, and Liz looked at the number on the caller ID.

It was Parker.

Liz was about to let the call go to voice mail, when her curiosity about what Parker might have to say got the better of her. Did he even *know* he had been a complete and total jerk?

"Hello?" she answered.

"I'm so sorry," Parker said.

Just hearing his voice, Liz felt herself go soft. *At least he knows he's in trouble.* Then she shook her head. *Stay strong. Don't let him get away with treating you like crap.*

"I was a jackass at the party," he continued. "I went to take a phone call, and I got a little stoned, and I guess it made me really inconsiderate."

"Well, yeah . . ." Liz said. She shut her eyes, wishing she could be more confrontational. *What is it about him that gets to me so totally?*

"I know, I know. I don't blame you for being furious," Parker went on. "I mean, I'd hate it if you brought me to a party where I hardly knew anyone and then *you* got all caught up in talking to other people."

"I wouldn't do that, Parker," Liz said. There. That was sticking up for herself.

"That's because you're an unbelievably fantastic human being, and I'm just pond scum," Parker said. "Well, all the ponds are frozen over right now, so I guess maybe I'm more like snow slush. Oh—and did I say that you are not just an angel, a saint, and a delight, you're a hot dancer and very, *very* forgiving?"

Liz smiled, and then forced herself to not give in to Parker's charm so fast. The only way to not melt completely would be to hang up. "Look, Parker, I have to go," she said.

"Liz, wait!" Parker said. "I need to see you."

"I can't, Parker. I'm taking the kids skating. Bye."

Liz hung up, and quickly dialed Adrienne.

"Is it good news or bad news?" Adrienne asked when she answered.

"Both," Liz said.

"Explain," Adrienne ordered.

Liz quickly filled in Adrienne on the details. "So some of the time he is totally great and makes me feel like I'm the most special person on Earth. And then he gets completely distracted by his crowd, ignores me and, worse, may have something going with Isabelle. And yet he called me and apologized." Liz sighed. "So do I forgive him? Or do I dump him?"

"Is that what you want to do?" Adrienne asked. "End it completely?"

"No," she said in a small voice. "But I can't stand this hot-and-cold treatment."

"I know," Adrienne said sympathetically. "It's really confusing."

"So what do you think?" Liz asked.

Adrienne paused as if she was thinking it over. "It's hard to say," she said finally. "Like you said, sometimes he's so great to you. But, Liz is *sometimes* enough?"

Liz squeezed her eyes shut, and her throat felt tight. "I don't know," she said, her voice quavering as if she was about to cry. "When it's good, it's"—Liz searched for the right word to describe the incredible times she'd had with Parker—"it's almost unreal. Like a fairy-tale dream come true."

"You like this guy in a way I've never seen you like anyone," Adrienne said. "Maybe you *should* give him a chance. He does seem to really like you, too."

"You think so?" Liz asked, starting to feel a glimmer of hope. "I just can't tell anymore."

"Look," Adrienne said. "He told you he hadn't seen this crowd for a while, that he was catching up with old friends. And it wasn't like he was trying to keep you a secret."

"That's true," Liz said, considering. Then she sighed. "But he did get all weird again when Isabelle showed up."

"You don't really know what's going on. It could be innocent. Well," Adrienne added with a laugh, "as innocent as anything can be with Isabelle around."

"Yeah, that's what worries me. Maybe he's hanging with her because she's happy to have sex whenever," Liz said. "As I hear it, she's happy to do it with *any* guy from Dudley."

"Don't even go there," Adrienne said. "And if that's all that Parker is after, you don't want him anyway. Besides, he's never pushed that, right?"

"Right," Liz agreed.

"So even if there *is* something like that going on with Isabelle, it probably doesn't mean anything."

"You think?" Liz asked, desperately wanting to believe her friend.

"It's not like you don't turn him on," Adrienne reminded Liz. "The heat between you is off-the-charts."

Liz smiled. "You noticed?"

Adrienne laughed. "How could I not? So obviously he's not pushing it because he takes you seriously."

"We need some hard-core girl-time when I get back," Liz said. "I see a lot of complaining, bitching, and moaning in our future!"

"Sounds like a New Year's party to me!"

"Grumpus and I are ready to go!" David shouted as he barreled back into the room.

"Gotta go. Grumpus calls," Liz said.

―――――――――

Liz was actually able to put the whole Parker question out of her mind and enjoy skating. The kids even got along well, though when Heather asked David if Grumpus was tired, Liz worried that the invisible-friend syndrome was contagious.

"I don't know about Grumpus," Liz said, "but I'm ready for a break!"

They ducked into the little rink café and Liz ordered a round of hot chocolates. Settling at a table, Liz had just taken a sip of her eight-dollar cocoa when a pair of hands covered her eyes. "Who is it?" Liz asked, though she knew.

The hands released, and a bouquet of stunning red roses appeared in front of her. An origami snowman poked out of the flowers and was holding a card that read, I'M SORRY.

"Parker—" Liz began.

"Just one more chance," Parker said, coming around to face her. "It's your last night in Aspen. Please let me take you out."

"Let him!" Heather said.

"Yeah, let him," David said.

"See?" Parker said. "I have allies who recognize my good qualities. I do have some, you know. Though they may not have been apparent last night."

Liz sighed. He really was hard to resist. "Okay," she agreed. "But only as a favor to the kids. I'd hate to disappoint them."

"Oh no, you couldn't do that," Parker said with a grin.

"I'll have to let Dr. Markham-Collins know," Liz said.

"But it shouldn't be a problem. The kids are going caroling, and she plans to join them."

The caroling was a major Aspen event, it seemed, and anyone who was *anyone* brought their kids, and if they didn't have any, they tried to borrow them.

"Why don't we plan for around eight o'clock, but call me so I know you're ready to go." He kissed her on the cheek and put the roses on the table beside her. "We'll go someplace quiet and romantic. I promise I will make it all up to you."

Liz touched one of the soft rose petals as Parker left. "They are pretty," she said. "I do love roses."

"Grumpus hates them," David said matter-of-factly. "They have thorns."

Liz snorted. "You know," she said, "I think we could probably all learn a lot from Grumpus."

Dr. M-C okayed the date, but asked Liz to deal with the kids until they were ready to leave for caroling.

David decided to occupy himself by skiing in and out of the house—back and forth, back and forth, back and forth. Liz had gotten nearly hypnotized just watching him, so she went up to her room to change.

"Not bad," she murmured, admiring herself in the narrow mirror. She wore a black silk top from Etro that she had borrowed from Adrienne, a pale pink skirt she'd splurged on a few months back, and a beautiful pair of Jimmy Choos that Dr. M-C had broken and thrown out. Liz had had them fixed and kept them.

Determining she was ready, Liz went downstairs.

"You look very nice," Dr. M-C said. "Kids, come say good-bye to Liz."

Heather and David came into the enormous living room.

"I'm going out tonight," Liz explained, "and I'm leaving really early tomorrow morning to go back to New York. I might be gone before you wake up, so have a wonderful Christmas." She handed them each a big wrapped box to put under their Christmas tree. She had bought them toys they had pointed out during their last trip to FAO Schwarz. She had even gotten Grumpus a toy, too! That scored big points with Dr. M-C., Liz noted.

"Thanks," Heather said. "Merry Christmas!" She gave Liz a tight hug.

"But who will stay with me and Grumpus?" David asked.

"Well, you'll have Billie and your mom."

"I'll miss you!" David said, giving her an awkward hug since he was still wearing his skis. "And Grumpus will miss you too!" He skied back outside again.

Liz went into the kitchen to let Billie know she was leaving, when Dr. M-C came dashing in.

"Come quickly!" she shrieked. "There's been a terrible accident!"

"What?" Liz gasped. She could hear David shrieking as if he were in agony. "Oh, no!" Liz ran after Dr. M-C and out the door that David had just skied out of, Billie following right behind them.

David was screaming and crying, pointing at the snow. Dr. M-C was hysterical, waving her arms and running around. Heather stared at the scene with horror.

"What's wrong?" Liz asked, running over to David. She knelt down in the snow and grabbed his shoulders. "Are you hurt?"

"Grumpus broke his leg skiing!" David screamed.

Liz's eyes nearly bugged out of her head. "You have got to be kidding me!" Liz said, turning to Dr. M-C. *If these shoes and this skirt are ruined, I may have to kill someone,* she thought.

"We all must go to the hospital now!" Dr. M-C ordered.

Liz stood up and brushed the snow from her knees. "What?"

"We have a child with a broken leg. Of course, we must find a doctor!" Dr. M-C said.

"But we don't!" Liz said. "We have a child who—"

"NEEDS TO GO TO THE HOSPITAL, ELIZABETH!" Dr. M-C hollered.

I give up. The woman is insane.

Dr. M-C ran to where David lay, weeping on the snow. Billie had dropped a blanket on him. Heather sat nearby, transfixed. "Billie, you stay here with Heather. Liz, David, and I will take Grumpus to the hospital."

"But I can't go!" Liz blurted. "I have a date!"

"Grumpus needs you, Liz!" Dr. M-C said, hurrying into the house. She returned wearing her sable coat and helped David and Grumpus into the back of the Mercedes SUV. "Come quickly, Liz!"

Liz hesitated. She looked at her watch. Parker was expecting her to call soon.

Dr. M-C hurried over to Liz. "Elizabeth, we all need to cooperate at a time like this," she said in a warning tone.

Liz sighed as she slid into the passenger seat, and Dr. M-C hit the gas. She might still be able to get back in time to meet Parker, she reasoned. After all, how long could examining an invisible kid take?

The attending nurse in the Aspen General emergency room was in no mood to play along with the Markham-Collins Family Circus.

"Lady, there ain't no little boy with a broken leg. If you don't get out of here, I will call Psychiatric to come and take a look at you!"

"I am a *doctor* of psychiatry," Dr. M-C announced

grandly. "And I assure you that I am well-known to the members of your—"

"I don't care if you're Dr. Phil!" the woman said, folding her arms. "You're crazy, and you're wasting my time! I've got plenty of really sick people who need actual help, and I don't have time to listen to . . ."

Liz pressed her fingers to her temples. This whole stupid scene was giving her a headache. Everyone was staring at them as if they were freaks.

Liz glanced up. She just realized she hadn't heard David giving Grumpus-related instructions for a while.

That's because he wasn't in the waiting room. Liz scanned the crowded space. David was gone.

"David?" Liz called, nerves making her voice quiver. *Okay, don't panic. He was with us when we arrived. He probably hasn't left the building.*

She ran around the corner and looked down a corridor. "David?" she called again and again. She leaned against the wall to try to figure out what to do.

Keep searching.

Liz ran up and down corridors, trying to figure out where David might have gone. She wound up back in Admitting, where Dr. M-C and the nurse were still arguing.

"Dr. Markham-Collins!" Liz shouted to be heard over Dr. M-C's threats and proclamations. "I can't find David!"

Dr. M-C paused with her mouth open, looked at Liz,

then turned back to the nurse. "This is all your fault!" she screamed. "If you had paid proper attention to the situation, he never would have run away!"

"You want to know why that kid ran away?" the nurse replied. "Look in the mirror."

Dr. M-C reared back as if the woman had slapped her. Then her eyes narrowed. "We're talking lawsuit now," she hissed.

"Please," Liz said to the nurse. "Do you think you could ask Security to look for him?"

The nurse smiled at Liz. "Of course, hon," she said sweetly. It was as if she had become a different person.

"We must find David," Dr. M-C cried. "He must think we don't care about poor Grumpus!"

Liz began to search the halls again. She noticed the time on one of the hall clocks. She was already late for her date. She flipped open her cell phone. No service.

"Fine." She glared at the phone. "Be that way."

She tossed it back into her bag and raced down a hall that led to the cafeteria.

Of course. Contraband snacks. That's got to be where David is.

She pushed through the door and there he was, staring longingly at a vending machine. "David," said Liz. "Are you okay?"

"I'm hungry," he complained. "And I don't want you to go home."

"Oh, David, I have to see my family for Christmas," Liz said. "And I'll see you the minute you get back to New York." She kissed his head and ruffled his hair. "But you were very naughty sneaking away like this. You had me very worried."

"I'm sorry."

"Well, you're going to have to apologize to a few other people, too," Liz said. "So let's get back to where your mom is and tell them to stop searching for you."

"Okay," David said, taking her hand. Liz wished she had brought some money with her to buy him a snack.

They returned to the admitting station, where Dr. M-C was demanding a private room for Grumpus. The attending nurse had gone back to work and was just letting Dr. M-C rant and rave.

"Everything's fine," Liz announced. "I found him."

"Oh, David!" Dr. M-C gushed. "I know you were upset about poor Grumpus and that's why you ran away. Don't worry, Grumpus will be fine!"

"But, Mommy," David said. "Grumpus doesn't exist. I made him up. Can we go get ice cream now?"

Dr. M-C stared at David, straightened up to her full— and quite imposing height—shut her eyes, and took in a deep, slow breath. She looked as if she was trying not to faint. Or explode.

"Listen," Liz said, before Dr. M-C dragged her into

any more craziness. "I'm late for my date. Do you think you can drop me off at Parker's? I'll let him know I'm on my way."

Dr. M-C opened her eyes and shook her head as if to clear it. She focused on Liz. "All right," she said.

Once they left the hospital vicinity, Liz's phone worked again. Only now, all she got was Parker's voice mail. She left two messages, then finally tried the landline at the house.

"Devlin residence," an older woman answered.

"Hi there, I'm Liz," she said. "May I speak with Parker?"

"Master Parker just left," the woman said. "He and Miss Isabelle Schyuler have gone to the Caribou Club. He said he had made reservations for dinner. Perhaps you'll find him there."

Liz shut the phone and sank back into the seat. *Those were* our *reservations.* Our *romantic dinner. Only he's having it with Isabelle instead.*

CHAPTER SIXTEEN

payback time!

Back in New York, Liz sat at the counter of the Salad Patch between Jane and Belinda with her head down. She sighed as she finished the tale of her Aspen misadventure.

"What a disaster," Belinda said. "It must have totally ruined the rest of Christmas break for you."

"It did," Liz confided. "The day after Christmas, Adrienne and I went to Serendipity for frozen hot chocolate, and I just sat there."

"You turned down chocolate?" Jane asked. "*Now* I know this is serious."

"Didn't Parker understand you didn't mean to stand him up?" Belinda asked.

"I e-mailed him an apology after I got back, explaining the whole hospital mess, but all he wrote back was, 'No prob. Stuff happens.'" Liz moved her uneaten salad around on her plate. "He should have gotten back into town last weekend, but I haven't heard from him."

Loud giggling grabbed Liz's attention. She glanced down the counter to where a few girls from P-B sat staring at her. They immediately lowered their heads and giggled more quietly.

"What's with them?" Liz asked her friends.

Jane and Belinda glanced nervously at each other.

"What?" Liz asked, tension creeping through her entire body.

"Uh," Jane mumbled, her perma-cool completely ruined, "we didn't really want to tell you," she began.

"Because, of course, the rumors are, like, *totally* ridiculous," continued Belinda.

"What rumors?" Liz asked.

"Well . . ." Belinda hesitated.

"Well, what?" Liz practically shouted.

"Calm down!" Jane said. "It's no big deal, really. People are just kind of saying that you were screwing around with Parker because you're a social climber."

Liz's eyes widened. "How can anyone think that?" she asked, her voice trembling.

"They're also saying that the thing with Isabelle is serious, that Parker is just slumming with you." Belinda studied her paper napkin.

Now Liz's mouth dropped open.

"We know it's not true," Jane said.

"And that's what we told everyone else!" Belinda

nodded vigorously, her waves bouncing.

"Everyone?" Liz said faintly. "You mean, that's what *everyone* thinks?"

Just then, the little bells over the door chimed, and Cameron and Mimi sauntered into the restaurant. All heads turned, then a buzz of gossip took over the room like a swarm of bees.

"What are they doing here?" Liz asked. "They NEVER eat lunch here."

"But they know you do," Jane pointed out. "This is totally calculated."

The girls strolled to the counter and stopped directly behind Liz.

"Hi, Liz," Mimi said. "I was sorry you didn't stay longer in Aspen. It would have been fun to see you at the Red and White Ball."

"I'm sure," Liz said. She pulled out her money to pay. She wanted to get out of there—fast.

"You would have loved Parker's outfit," Cameron said. "He looked totally hot."

"And Isabelle!" Mimi gushed. "She looked drop-dead gorgeous."

"They made the cutest couple," Cameron agreed. "So perfect together."

"Cameron," Jane asked, swiveling around on her stool to face the girl, "are you this much of a bitch when you get

up every morning, or do you have to do warm-ups first?"
She stood up, and Liz stood beside her.

Cameron gave a smug smile and turned to Mimi.
"Some girls have such a hard time with jealousy."

"Some girls have an even harder time with their curtsy,"
Belinda said. "I hear that not even your trainer can stop you
from looking like a clown. The word is that Mimi's is much
better."

Cameron looked wounded. Mimi looked smug. Liz
and her friends strolled out of the Salad Patch, heads held
high.

"My curtsy is totally fine!" Liz heard Cameron whine
behind them.

Once they were outside, Jane, Belinda, and Liz burst
out laughing. Clutching one another to keep from top-
pling over, they headed back to school, laughing the whole
way. Finally they got control of themselves. Liz wiped her
eyes, not sure if the tears were from laughing or from being
so upset.

"Are you okay?" Jane asked gently.

"I'm better than okay," Liz replied. "I'm seriously angry."

"Why is angry good?" Belinda asked.

"Because when I'm mad, I go into action," Liz said.
"Instead of curling up into a little ball and whimpering."

"What kind of action do you have in mind?" Jane
asked.

"I'm going to find out once and for all what is going on with the whole 'Parker and Isabelle' thing."

"How?" Belinda asked.

"By observing them together in their natural habitat." Liz pulled out her phone and hit autodial.

"Adrienne?" Liz said. "I need to get into the Manhattan Cotillion next week. And *you* are going to help me."

After school that day, Liz and Adrienne argued over a soda at Viand Coffee Shop on Madison Avenue.

"No way!" Adrienne said. "Liz, you have lost your mind!"

"No, I haven't," Liz insisted. "This is a great idea. If I can just see Parker and Isabelle together, I'll know what's going on. I'll come right out and ask him—with Isabelle standing right there, if I have to."

"Liz," Adrienne said. "I applaud your proactive thinking, but we cannot crash the biggest social event of the year at the Plaza Hotel."

"So," Liz said, her eyes flashing, "the dance is at the *Plaza*!"

"Ohmigod." Adrienne smacked her forehead. "I *so* should not have said anything."

"It will be easy to get in," Liz pressed. "All we need to do is dress up, and we'll look like we belong there."

Adrienne frowned. Liz knew her friend was weakening.

"Besides," Liz continued, knowing which buttons to push, "don't you want to get between Cameron and Brian? You *know* you almost managed to make him forget that blond bitch when you had half a chance. It would be perfect justice if you could steal him away from her at the ball."

Adrienne bit her lip.

Great, Liz thought. *She's considering it.*

"Come on, Adrienne," Liz wheedled. "We'll slip in, I'll talk to Parker, you grab Brian, we push Mimi and Cameron down a flight of stairs, and bang, we're out of there."

"That sounds satisfying, but impractical," Adrienne said with a giggle. Then she groaned. "Please, Liz, I beg you, don't make me do this!"

Liz's shoulders slumped. "Adrienne, I can't keep going on like this," she confessed, all the bravado gone from her voice. "I have to figure out if Isabelle really is a threat. If Parker is serious about me or not. All of the gossip—"

"Forget the gossip," Adrienne said. She took in a deep breath and then let out a slow exhale. "All right!" she said. "Let's do it." She stood and grabbed her purse. "But to pull this off, you have to come with me."

"Where are we going?" Liz asked as she followed Adrienne out of the coffee shop.

"I have to stop by Valentino and pick up Cameron's dress," Adrienne explained. "If anyone can help us, it's Kevyn."

The girls practically ran the few short blocks to Valentino. Kevyn stood near the window, gazing forlornly at the street. He crossed to them as they burst through the glass doors.

"Hey there, sugar," Kevyn said, kissing Adrienne on both cheeks. "How are you?"

"I'm fine," Adrienne said, shaking the snow from her coat. "This is my friend, Liz Braun."

Kevyn nodded at Liz. "Welcome to our little shop."

"Is something wrong?" Adrienne asked. "You look awful."

"Well, *thank you*," Kevyn said, putting a hand on his hip. He shook his head. "You're lucky you didn't find me here with my head in the oven. What a day! That Cameron of yours is such a pain!"

"Believe me, she's not *my* Cameron," Adrienne said.

"What happened?" Liz asked.

"The ladies in the workroom worked their fingers to the bone getting the deb dress ready," Kevyn explained. "Valentino himself flew in to make sure every pearl and bead was perfect. Do you know that the Warners insisted on using *real* pearls on the dress? The work that went into it was incredible. And today, just as we're steaming out the wrinkles to pack it for you to pick up, we get a call from Mrs. Warner." Kevyn began a devastating impersonation of Mrs. Warner: "'Cameron isn't happy, the poor thing. And

after all, the dress *is* a little ostentatious, don't you think?'"
Kevyn sighed. "So they went to Vera Wang up the street
and bought something"—he shuddered—"off the rack!"

"No!" Adrienne gasped.

Liz fought back a laugh. Kevyn was extremely dramatic. It wasn't as if a dress was a matter of life and death.
Then again, she mused, *in* this *world, fashion somehow becomes
an earth-shattering issue.*

"Trust me, darling," Kevyn continued, "if it weren't for
the thirty-thousand-dollars' worth of pearls sewn to the
bodice of this dress, I would throw it into the street for the
buses to run over. Preferably while Cameron was still wearing it."

"We know just how you feel," Adrienne said.

Liz nodded. "We definitely relate. Cameron Warner
seems to be at the center of all the bad things that have
been happening to us lately."

"Do tell," Kevyn said.

"As you know, Cameron stole Adrienne's boyfriend,"
Liz said. "And now Cameron is helping one of her friends
put the moves on *my* guy. She just loves manipulating
everyone around her. Like a game."

"We need your help to get back at them," Adrienne
said.

"How?" Kevyn asked, obviously relishing the plan.

"We're going to crash the cotillion," Liz declared.

Kevyn smiled at them. "Get you two!"

"The biggest obstacle is getting in," Liz said. "And to do that, we have to look like we belong there."

"Can we borrow some clothes?" Adrienne asked. "Pretty please? We promise to be really careful."

"I have a better idea," Kevyn said. "You come here the night of the party and I will not only lend you fabulous gowns, but I'll get my friends together to get you ready for the ball. Hair, makeup, jewelry—the works!"

"You'd really do that?" Liz asked.

"Honey, I'm so annoyed with Cameron," he said, "I'd do anything to make certain that you two look better than she does! She needs someone to knock her off her little diamond pedestal."

Liz grinned. "Sounds like payback time to me."

CHAPTER SEVENTEEN

kicking debutante butt

"Cameron!" Mrs. Warner called, drawing on her long gray satin gloves. "Hurry! You can't be late for this!"

Adrienne stood in the hall of the Warners' apartment, waiting to be allowed to leave. She glanced at her watch again. She didn't have much time to get over to Valentino's to get ready.

I never should have let Liz talk me into this, she thought. She'd been getting more and more nervous as the day approached.

The elevator door opened, and Brian stepped in. It was the first time she'd seen him outside of French class since their abbreviated date during Christmas break. He looked handsome in his white tie and tails, but not very comfortable.

Mr. Warner walked in, a glass of scotch in his hand. "Oh," he said, seeing Brian. "You again."

"Adriana," Mrs. Warner said, her tone imperious. "Might I have a word with you?"

"Sure," Adrienne said, her heart sinking a bit. She knew Mrs. Warner was not pleased to see Brian—and that the COW would blame her.

They reached the dining room, and Mrs. Warner wheeled around. "I thought we had a deal!" she hissed. "What is that boy doing here?"

"Mrs. Warner," Adrienne said, "I'm doing the best I can. I'm still going to try to keep him from being presented with Cameron at the Plaza."

"I certainly hope you'll come through for us," Mrs. Warner said, straightening her diamond necklace. She turned and left the room.

Adrienne slowly returned to the hall. *Our plan just has to work*, she vowed.

Debi LaDeux appeared wearing a dress that looked straight out of the movie *Gone With the Wind*.

Either that or off the top of a wedding cake, Adrienne thought. Lace, ruffles, miles of tulle and ribbons made it seem as if Debi's dress were a living creature all on its own.

"Y'all," she drawled, her skirts rustling, "we have completed our project. Ladies and gentlemen, may I present Miss Cameron Warner!"

Cameron walked in slowly, with a bashful smile, eyes downcast. Her dress was incredible even if it *was* "off the rack." The cream satin bodice was fitted perfectly to her upper body, and had a cream piqué off-the-shoulder reverse-shawl collar. A strand of pale pink pearls gleamed softly around her neck and her hair was gathered into a low bun at the nape of her neck and decorated with jasmine blossoms. Her makeup was subtle, pale, and natural. She looked virginal and sweet.

Nothing like her real self at all.

"I hate this stupid dress," she complained, ruining the illusion. "It makes me look like a Disney character."

"Nonsense," Mrs. Warner said. "It's perfect. You look lovely, Cam."

"Absoluteluh Duh-VINE," Debi gushed. "Show them your curtsuh, daw-lin.'"

Cameron fell down into the much-practiced "Texas dip." Everyone applauded except for Adrienne. She resisted giving Cameron a push. She looked pretty easy to topple.

"Get up, honey," Mr. Warner said. "Time to go."

"I can't," Cameron complained from the floor. "The skirt is really heavy."

"It's interlined," Mrs. Warner said. "The dress at Valentino wasn't. He warned us about this."

"Well, why didn't you listen?" Cameron whined, swimming in satin.

"You were the one who insisted on changing dresses!" Mrs. Warner snapped. "Perhaps you should have listened to *me* for once!"

"Don't worry, Cam-sweetie," Debi said, pushing Brian

forward. "Your escort will help you up."

Brian gave his hand to Cameron, who leaned heavily on it and pulled herself up.

Adrienne smirked. *Way to be graceful, Cam-sweetie.*

"Okay." Mr. Warner downed his scotch. "Get Emma. We're off."

Adrienne went to Emma's room, where the little girl sat watching a taped *Face the Nation* on TV. She looked adorable in a tiny pink Valentino frock.

"Hey, Emma," Adrienne said. "Time to go to the ball."

Emma rolled her eyes and brushed wrinkles from her skirt as she stood. "Must I go?"

Adrienne nodded. "You must."

"I depart," Emma said. "Though not without acute reservations."

Adrienne brought Emma to the hall, and the Warners gathered for a picture taken by a *Vogue* photographer, thanks to editor in chief Anna Wintour, one of Mrs. Warner's best friends.

Finally, Adrienne thought, as the elevator doors shut on the Warner family. She pulled out her cell. "They're gone. We have one hour."

"Meet you downstairs," Liz said.

The two girls met on Fifth Avenue and raced over to Valentino on Madison. Kevyn paced in front of the door.

The moment he saw the girls, he unlocked it and yanked it open.

"Hurry," he ordered. "Run to the back! Run, run, run!"

The girls dashed to the dressing room area. Three fashionistas stood waiting for them.

"Girls," Kevyn announced, "this is Linda, who'll do your hair." A skinny woman with beautifully high-lighted chestnut hair nodded. "Leslie, who'll do your makeup." A very thin, androgynous-looking person with a buzz cut, nearly invisible makeup, and baggy clothes stepped forward. Now Kevyn placed his hands on the shoulders of a tall black man. "And this is Jake, who'll do the styling."

"Thanks everyone," Liz said.

"Your dresses are already hung in the changing rooms," Kevyn said. "Now go!"

Liz stepped into one of the changing rooms, and began undressing.

"You can't wear a bra with that dress," Jake declared as he slipped into the booth with her.

"Hey!" Liz said. "I'm changing in here!"

"Chill out, honey," he said. "You can't do this by yourself. Don't worry, my eyes are closed. Take off your bra, step into the dress, and let me know when you are decent."

Liz stripped and stepped into the dress, pulling it up

around her. *This is bizarre. I'm not exactly used to having some guy help dress me!*

Jake tugged a lot at the back of the dress. Finally he stepped back and announced, "You're good. Go out for hair and makeup."

Adrienne forced herself not to flinch while Linda tortured her with various curling wands and other wicked-looking devices. She couldn't help wondering if she'd wind up looking like a poodle.

"Just a few seconds more," said Linda, "and you're done."

Adrienne turned to the mirror. Her hair was piled on top of her head and was softly curling around her ears and spilling down the back of her neck. "Will it stay?" she asked Linda, afraid that putting on the dress would mess up the gorgeous style.

"It will take two showers to wash out all this silicone, trust me," Linda said, grinning. "Now go change."

The two girls met in the hallway, and neither could believe their eyes.

Liz had never seen Adrienne so beautiful. Her friend actually seemed to glow. The pale peach dress, encrusted with crystals and pearls, was the perfect color for her complexion. Her titian-colored hair framed her face romantically, and her subtle makeup made her pure competition for Cameron.

Adrienne admired Liz's stark white dress, which brought out her dark eyes and pretty collarbones. Her hair was pulled back in a glossy, sleek style, emphasizing her cheekbones. She dripped sophistication and glamour.

Kevyn applauded excitedly, gushing and complimenting everyone. "Now," he added, grinning, "the pièce de résistance: This is my friend Kyoko from Mikimoto."

A slender Japanese woman stepped forward and opened two beautiful boxes, each of which contained a fabulous pearl necklace.

"Only pearls are right for debutantes," Kyoko announced. "You can return them later."

"Are you serious?" Adrienne asked, her eyes wide.

"Go ahead!" Kevyn urged, clasping the lustrous pearls around Adrienne's neck.

"I feel like I'm about to get married," Liz said, adjusting her voluminous skirts.

"*I* feel like I'm about to yak," Adrienne said with a gulp. "I can't believe we're really doing this."

"You're both going to be fine," Kevyn insisted. "Now go to the Plaza Hotel and kick some debutante butt!"

CHAPTER EIGHTEEN

at the Plaza

Adrienne and Liz slowly climbed the plush, red-carpeted stairs of the Plaza Hotel. They shivered in the winter air, but the heating lamps under the stained-glass and bronze canopy were warm and inviting.

People swept aside to let them pass, smiling and nodding. One man even asked to take their picture.

It's working, Liz thought. *They actually think we belong here.*

The doormen held open the wide doors on either side of the revolving door, to prevent their long gowns from getting stuck in the spinning central door. Entering the lavishly gilded lobby, with its ornate mosaic floor covered by heavy plush carpets, Liz inhaled the warm air scented with the pleasant combination of furniture polish and fresh roses. In the Palm Court, dozens of couples dined at little tables, listening to the swirling music of violins and harps.

"Do you know where we're going?" Liz asked Adrienne.

"Nope," Adrienne replied. "Look for signs for the Grand Ballroom." Suddenly, Adrienne gasped and turned, holding a hand up to hide her face.

"What is it?" Liz asked, panicked.

"It's Debi LaDeux!" Adrienne whispered. "She's totally going to recognize me!"

"Girls!" Debi said, furious, her petticoats aflutter as she approached. "What aw you doing he-uh?"

Adrienne's grip on Liz's arm tightened. She kept her back to Debi and stared at Liz with an expression like a deer caught in headlights.

"Uh, we uh, we were just going . . ." Liz sputtered.

"To the Grand Ballroom, I hope!" Debi said. "The presentation is about ten minutes away! RUN!" she shrieked, waving her clipboard down the hall.

"I guess we'd better hurry," Liz said. "Come on!"

The girls hurried toward the back of the hotel. Now that Debi had pointed them in the right direction, it was easy to follow the gilded signs to the Grand Ballroom.

Adrienne and Liz scurried up the long, wide flight of marble steps to the second floor and then found their way into a marble vestibule that glittered with crystal and gilt bronze.

"Not this way, girls," a woman behind a linen-swathed

table instructed. "I'm checking in the guests. The debutantes are meeting in the Baroque Room. You have to check in there." She frowned. "They won't let you in without your escorts, though. I trust they'll be here soon?"

"Of course!" Liz bluffed. She grabbed Adrienne's hand. "We don't want to be late." She practically dragged Adrienne down the carpeted corridor.

"Where are we going now?" Adrienne hissed.

"To the Baroque Room, of course," Liz said, turning the corner. "Because if that's where the debs are, that's where we'll find Parker and Brian."

"We won't be able to get in," Adrienne said, coming to a complete stop. "That woman just said we need escorts. We'll have to figure out something else to do."

Suddenly, Adrienne felt a hand on the small of her back.

"So, you followed me here?" she heard a deep voice say. "I knew you couldn't resist me."

Adrienne turned around. *Graydon*. "What are you doing here?" she asked, shaking off his hand.

"My pal and I decided to check out the debs. Oh, and to support my sister, of course."

"Of course," Adrienne said.

Graydon's friend smirked at the girls. "Why aren't you introducing me, Gray?" Liz thought both guys seemed pretty tipsy.

"Sooooooooo sorry," Graydon said. "Girls, *please* meet

Albright N. Smiley the third. His mother is Lady Anabelle Browne-Fowlkes. She's related to Prince Charles." He slung his arm across Adrienne's shoulder and leaned heavily on her. "Impressed?"

"Back off, you creep," Adrienne said, trying to pull away from Graydon.

Graydon grinned at Albright, who was staring at Liz as if she were candy. "She just loves to play hard-to-get. That really turns me on."

"I'm not playing," Adrienne said, slipping out from under his arm. He stumbled, but caught himself before he spilled his champagne. *That would be perfect*, Adrienne thought. *Graydon splashing this hundred-thousand-dollar dress with booze!* She stepped farther away from him.

Liz clutched Adrienne's arm. "I have an idea," she whispered. "They can get us back there!"

"What?" Adrienne asked.

"They can pretend to be our escorts," Liz explained. "The woman at the door is sure to know them and will let them in."

She's right, Adrienne realized. She turned to Graydon. As much as she hated to do it, she had to ask him for the favor. "Can you take Liz and me back to see Cam?"

"We want to wish her luck," Liz added.

"What's in it for me?" Graydon asked, leering at Adrienne.

"I'll dance with you," Adrienne replied.

He laughed. "Not good enough," he said, swigging his champagne. "I want a date."

A DATE? Just thinking about it made her skin crawl. "No way," Adrienne said.

"Hang on a sec," Liz said to Graydon. She dragged Adrienne a few feet away from the guys. "It's just one date!" she begged.

Adrienne stared at her. "Liz, he's a complete and total pig!" she said. "You don't know what you're asking."

"It's our only shot at getting in," Liz pleaded. "How bad could one date be?"

Adrienne looked at Liz's pleading expression and sighed. *One date,* she thought. *I can live through that. Probably.*

"Okay," she said. "But don't leave me alone with him tonight. And you owe me big."

"Thank you," Liz said, relief flooding her face. She hadn't come this far to be stopped by her lack of an escort.

Adrienne, Graydon, Albright, and Liz headed to the Baroque Room. Another woman with a clipboard stood outside the door. "And you are?" she asked, gazing at Adrienne and Liz and then back down at her notes.

"Mrs. Smithon!" Graydon greeted the gray-haired woman. "We missed you in Palm Beach!"

"Why, Graydon, darling," the woman gushed, holding her powdered cheek toward Graydon, who obligingly kissed it. "I hadn't realized you were one of the escorts this evening."

"What's a Manhattan Cotillion without a few surprises?" Gradyon said, his expression completely sweet while he slid his hand toward Adrienne's rear.

She stepped forward quickly and out of his reach. "We don't want to be late!" she said, and charged through the door. Liz followed right behind her.

"We made it in," Liz whispered to Adrienne. She gazed around the gold and white room. Seven beautifully dressed girls and their escorts frantically checked mirrors, powdered their noses, and whispered nervously. She noticed Mimi's escort, but no Mimi—or Parker.

As Liz and Adrienne moved deeper into the room, Adrienne noticed that all the girls and several of their escorts were staring at her. *Do they know we're crashing the party?* she wondered. Some of them had seen her at Cameron's tea and probably knew she was the nanny.

"Why are they staring?" she asked Liz anxiously.

"Oh, I don't know, Adrienne," Liz replied, laughing. "Like, maybe it is the TENS OF THOUSANDS of dollars' worth of pearls sewn to your dress and around your neck?"

"Oh, right," Adrienne said, glancing down at her dress. "I forgot."

A slim, older woman with ash-blond hair clapped her hands. "Ladies, ladies. And gentlemen, of course," she added with a smile. "I'm Mrs. Heusen and I going to put you in order and go over your introduction cards. Then I'll give your cards to our host, who will make your announcements." She glanced down at her cards and looked around the room. "We seem to missing some of our debutantes."

"Maybe we should try to make ourselves invisible," Liz whispered to Adrienne, slinking behind Graydon and Albright. "We don't want to get thrown out before we see Brian and Parker."

Just then, Cameron, Mimi, and Isabelle breezed in. Cameron's eyes landed on Adrienne. Her gray eyes traveled up and down the peach Valentino dress and then narrowed.

"Uh-oh," Adrienne said, ducking behind Albright to stand beside Liz. "Cam just spotted me."

"So what?" Liz said, scanning the room for Parker.

"So this is officially war, Liz," Adrienne said. "I hope you know what you are doing."

Liz hoped she did too.

"Okay, let's go through your introduction cards," Mrs. Heusen said. "Please stand with your escorts."

"Showtime!" Cameron said as Parker and Brian came in through the door.

Liz's heart clutched a little when she spotted Parker. She ducked behind Adrienne, suddenly not wanting him to see her. Now that she was here, she was less certain about what she should do.

The debs and their escorts paired up, and Mrs. Heusen circulated through the room, reading the cards and putting everyone in order.

"We're just here to give our support," Graydon told the woman as she flipped through the cards, trying to find his name. "As you know, Cameron Warner is my half sister."

"Oh, yes, of course," Mrs. Heusen said. "You really shouldn't be back here, but since your stepmother *is* the ball chairwoman, I'll make an exception. Now, speaking of Miss Cameron?"

Cameron stepped forward, pulling Brian with her. Mrs. Heusen looked down at Cameron's card. "Is this correct?" she asked, sounding puzzled. "All it says here for your escort's introduction is 'Brian Grady.'"

"That's my name," Brian said.

"Yes, darling, and a very nice one it is, too, but there's nothing here about your progenitors, your family."

"Like what?" Brian asked.

Now the woman looked even more confused. "The usual: titles, family origins, genealogy . . ."

Cameron's forehead wrinkled. The questions were obviously making her even more uncomfortable than they were making Brian. "Uh, Brian's family prefers to stay out of the limelight. Discretion, and all that. You know . . ." she trailed off.

"Well, all right," Mrs. Heusen said uncertainly. She

moved on to Mimi and her archduke. "Mimi, could you just read this through and make sure I haven't left out any of the royal or imperial titles belonging to you or your charming escort?"

Once Mimi had given Mrs. Heusen her nod of approval, the woman dashed out to the stage with the cards. Suddenly, the waltz that had been playing stopped, and Mrs. Warner's voice rang out over the sound system.

"Thank you, everyone. Thank you so, so, so much for coming," Mrs. Warner said, adjusting the microphone with a minimum of feedback.

"I would like to introduce you to the man who has covered New York society for so many years for the *New York Times*, Mr. John Addison, who will announce this year's class of debutantes at the Manhattan Cotillion."

"Girls!" Mrs. Heusen said. "Quickly, we're starting. Mimi, you're first!"

Now Mr. Addison's voice could be heard over the loudspeaker.

"Get out of my way!" said Mimi, pushing past her friends. "He's calling my name!"

"Her Serene Highness, Princess Maria Augusta Victoria Ludmila Gertrude von Fallschirm, with her escort, His Royal and Imperial Highness Archduke Rudolph-Heinz von Habsburg, Prince of Hungary, of Teplitz . . . "

Adrienne tuned out the announcement and focused on Cameron. With every title of Mimi's or Rudolph's the reporter announced, the more miserable Cameron looked.

"I should have listened to my stepmother," Cameron said to Brian. "This is horrible. A reporter from the *Times* is here, and I'm with you! Mimi has an archduke, Isabelle has Parker, and I have *you*. A nobody!"

"Cam, that's so rude!" Isabelle said, shocked.

"Now, Isabelle and Parker," Mrs. Heusen ordered. "Go!"

Isabelle squealed and rushed to the doorway. "Parker, come on!" she said.

Liz glanced to the back of the room and saw Parker on his cell. *I guess he takes calls when he's with Isabelle, too,* she thought.

Parker clicked off and headed toward Isabelle, who was standing near the door.

I'm so confused about him, Liz thought, watching him approach. *Why does he have to be so cute?*

As he passed Liz, he suddenly caught sight of her. His mouth dropped open, and then he smiled at her. "You look *beautiful,*" he said.

"Parker!" Isabelle whined. "Hurry up."

"I've missed you," he told Liz. "See you out there, okay?" He joined Isabelle at the door, and Mr. Addison announced them—and all of their family connections—as they stepped onto the stage. The crowd burst into applause as Isabelle dropped into her curtsy.

Liz turned to Adrienne. "I'm going out to the ball-room. I'm going to grab Parker when he comes off the stage with Isabelle," she said. She thought it was a really good sign that he had stopped to speak to her in front of everybody while Isabelle stood and waited for him.

"Go get him!" Adrienne said. "I need to stay here." She glanced over at Brian, who looked miserable. Cameron didn't look so happy herself.

"Good luck," Liz said, and then vanished.

Debi LaDeux pushed her way in. "Cameron?" she called, peering anxiously around the room. "Ah, there you are!" She rushed to Cameron's side. "I just wanted to give you a few little reminders before you went out there! After all, as your consultant, your performance reflects on me."

Mr. Addision announced another couple with a long list of impressive titles.

"Do you hear those announcements?" Cameron said. She gestured toward Brian. "All his card has on it is his stupid name!"

"Cameron!" Debi scolded. "They might hear you out in the ballroom!"

"But—" Brian said.

Cameron put her gloved hands on her hips. "Debi, I'm Cameron Warner," she whispered, "and I am *not* going out there with a nobody!"

"It's a little late to come to your senses now, de-ah," Debi clucked.

Now Brian stared at Debi. "But—" he began.

Cameron and Debi both continued to ignore him. Cam gazed around the room, completely panicked. She spotted Albright N. Smiley III. "You!" she called to him. "You're a friend of Graydon's?"

"Since our boarding school years," Albright said.

"Albright is even richer than we are," Graydon added, laughing.

"That's more than you can say," Cameron tossed at Brian.

Brian looked startled, then down at his feet.

She is unbelievable! Adrienne thought, her whole body growing warm with anger. She glanced at Brian. *Why won't he stand up to her?*

"You want to rescue me from making a huge mistake?" Cameron asked Albright, tipping her head toward Brian.

That's it! "Hey, Cameron," Adrienne said, stepping forward. "Brian wouldn't go out on that stage with you if you were the last deb on Earth." She took his hand. "Right, Bri?"

Brian stared at her. "What? Oh, right."

"Whatever, Nanny," Cameron said. "Take him. He's no good to me here." She turned to Albright. "What's your last name again?"

"Smiley," he said, grinning.

"Doesn't your family own Mediacorp International?"

"That's us," he said.

"Isn't your mom sort of a royal?" she asked.

Albright nodded.

"Good enough for me. Come on!" she said. She grabbed his hand. "Debi!" she ordered. "Change that card!"

Debi raced to Mrs. Heusen, grabbed the woman's pen, and scribbled the notes Albright dictated. Mr. Addison was still announcing the other debs and their escorts. Debi shoved the card into Mrs. Heusen's hand and pushed the startled woman onstage.

"And now for our final debutante," Mr. Addison said over the sound system. "May I present Miss Cameron Warner and her escort, Albright N. Smiley the third, son of Albright N. Smiley junior, of the Denver Smileys, and his wife, Anabelle, the former Lady Browne-Fowlkes of London."

"There *is* a God," Debi murmured, listening to the applause.

Brian squeezed Adrienne's hand. "It was great of you to stick up for me," he said. "You were totally right. I never should have been with Cameron. You're the only girl for me." He leaned toward her and kissed her.

As Adrienne felt his lips on hers she realized something strange. No familiar tingle. No weak knees. No wishing to pull him closer, to melt into him.

She didn't want him anymore.

"Adrienne," Brain said, pulling away to look at her. "What's wrong? I thought you wanted us to get back together."

Adrienne studied his face. If Brian had chosen her over Cameron, she might have felt differently. Instead, Cam had dumped him, and only now was he turning to her. And, she had seen him cave to Cameron *twice*. She shook her head.

"You know what, Brian?" Adrienne said. "I care about you, and I couldn't stand there and watch Cameron treat you like dirt. But I didn't deserve to be treated the way you treated me, either. I think *you* were right: We do need a break from each other."

Adrienne went out to the ornate ballroom, feeling better than she had for a long time.

Liz stared around the ballroom, barely able to take it all in. The high, gilded ceilings had huge glimmering chandeliers, and were filled with pale silver balloons dangling long golden ribbons that stretched almost to the large polished dance floor. The room was full of men with white tie and tails, and women wearing long ball gowns dripping with expensive jewels. The linen-draped tables were covered with tall bouquets of white roses, giving one the impression of being lost in an forest of flowers. It was like stepping into a fantasy.

She suddenly felt a tap on her shoulder. It was Parker.

"I didn't know you were coming," he said with a dazzling smile.

"Neither did I," she admitted. She took a deep breath. This is what she had come for, after all. "Okay, just tell it to me straight: Are you going out with Isabelle?"

Parker looked surprised. "No way! Liz, look at Isabelle!" He pointed to a corner, where Liz saw Isabelle making out with Mimi's archduke! Mouth open in shock, Liz turned back to Parker.

"Is Isabelle the reason you've been so weird?" Parker asked.

"Me?" Liz said.

"Yeah. I've barely heard from you since I got back."

"But—but," Liz sputtered.

"Liz, I *really* like you," Parker said, touching her cheek.

"You do?" Liz responded, feeling her heart flutter.

"Of course, I do," Parker said.

"Oh," Liz said, her voice soft. This was going *way* better than she had hoped! Before she completely fell under the Parker spell, she shook her head to clear it. "But all those calls," she said. "You're always on that cell. It makes me wonder if—"

Parker cut her off. "It's rude. I know." He shrugged. "What can I say? I'm too popular for my own good. It's a burden I try to live with."

Liz giggled and smacked his arm. "Shut up."

Parker laughed too, and pretended to protect himself from further attack. "Okay, so sometimes I can be a jerk—but at least I know it!"

"Can you try to know it in advance?" Liz said. "And then do a preemptive strike to avoid the jerkiness?"

"I'll do the best I can," Parker said, and grinned. "But no guarantees. I mean, you're asking me to change lifelong habits!"

He put on such a pathetic look, Liz burst out laughing.

He took her hand in his. "Come on, let's get out of here and get a slice of pizza."

"Dressed like this?"

"Of course!" Parker said. "After all the gourmet food shoved down my throat during the holidays, pizza is a *real* special occasion!"

He put his arm around Liz, and she leaned against him. *It was definitely worth coming here*, she thought. *The rumors are just rumors, and Parker really does like me. I can feel it.*

Adrienne looked around the ballroom, searching for Liz. The first person she saw, though, was Mrs. Warner.

"Oh, Adriana!" the woman gushed. She placed her hands on Adrienne's shoulders and kissed her on both cheeks. "You are genius! Absolute genius!"

"I—what?" Adrienne asked.

"I don't know how you did it, but I never should have

doubted you! You kept Cameron from making a complete and utter fool of herself with that Byron boy. And Albright Smiley the third! What a perfect escort!"

"Oh, right," Adrienne said. "Well, glad to have been of help."

"You are an angel. And don't you worry, that bonus is yours! It will be waiting for you back at the apartment. We Warners don't forget those who help us.

"Oh, they need me onstage," Mrs. Warner said, practically giddy. "Ta-ta, dear!" She disappeared into the elegant crowd.

"Ladies and gentlemen," Mr. Addison announced from the stage. "As you all know, every year we pick the debutante who exhibits the most perfect combination of birth, breeding, and beauty as Debutante of the Year. The competition was very close, but we are pleased to announce that the Debutante of the Year is . . . Princess Mimi von Fallschirm!"

This party just gets better, Adrienne thought with a grin.

As the crowd burst into applause, Cameron appeared beside her.

"That dress looks great on you, Adrienne," Cameron commented.

"What do *you* want, Cameron?" Adrienne said.

"Hey, no hard feelings," Cameron said. "You have Brian back."

"Don't want him anymore," Adrienne said. "And I have nothing to say to you."

"Don't be silly, Adrienne," Cameron said, moving closer. "I have a little proposal for you. And I know you won't be able to say no."

Adrienne faced Cameron. A slow, confident smile spread across Adrienne's face. "Trust me, Cameron. I can say no to you."

"No, you can't," Cameron said, her eyes glittering. "*I* was supposed to be Deb of the Year, Adrienne, and I'm going to get even with Mimi for this."

"That's between you and Mimi, Cam," Adrienne said, turning to walk away.

"Not if you want things to work out for Liz," Cameron called.

Adrienne stopped and slowly turned around. Now it was Cam who had the knowing smile.

"I know something about Parker that your friend will want to know before she gets any more involved with him," Cameron said.

"What's that, Cameron?" Adrienne demanded, hating that Cameron had her hooked this way. But she had to find out—for Liz's sake.

"I'll tell you, Adrienne. But only after I get even with Mimi—and you are going to help me do it!"

Look for Victoria Ashton's next novel,
CONFESSIONS OF A TEEN NANNY:
Juicy Secrets

"That was a great party Tamara had," Liz said to Adrienne. "Too bad there isn't another party this weekend!"

"You got that right," Adrienne said. Last Saturday, Adrienne and her pals had partied long into the night with wild dancing and massive amounts of takeout food at Tamara Tucker's apartment on the Upper West Side. It was the first time since their breakup that Adrienne had seen her ex-boyfriend Brian Grady outside of school. What had made it even more significant was that the party had a Valentine's Day theme—Adrienne's first Valentine's Day solo in two years. At first she'd been afraid she'd get all weepy, but instead she had laughed, danced, and scarfed down delicious veggie dumplings. "That party rocked."

"For you," Liz said, giggling. "I don't think it was so cool for Brian. He was totally mooning over you."

Adrienne grinned. "So you noticed, too?"

"Please. He may have dumped you first, but now the tables are seriously turned."

"No joke," Adrienne agreed. "I never thought it was possible, but I really am so totally over him."

"It's great to hear you say that," Liz said. "I was pretty worried about you there for a while."

"Me, too," Adrienne admitted. "But I'm great now. No guys stressing me out." She glanced over at Emma, Heather, and David. They were all busy with the markers and paper Liz had brought with her. "How's Parker doing?" Adrienne asked her friend quietly.

Liz shrugged.

Parker Devlin and Liz had been seeing each other for a few months, and Adrienne had never seen Liz go for a guy the way she was gone over Parker.

"What happened?" Adrienne asked. "You have that look again. Whenever you scrunch up your face, I know you're upset."

"Nothing. Nothing happened," Liz confided. "I guess that's the problem. With Parker, it's hard to tell where things stand. It's just that he hasn't been around much this week. And he wouldn't come to Tamara's party with me."

"Maybe he's busy with school," Adrienne suggested, although she seriously doubted that was the case.

"Probably. But Parker is always busy with something.

We have these really great dates—and then he drops off the planet for several days. I mean, don't you think he'd want to spend his time with *me*?" Liz said. "I want to spend *all* my time with him. He's so hot!"

"Guys are totally different from us," Adrienne said.

Liz nodded. "And rich guys are *way* different. Parker and Cameron aren't like normal kids."

Adrienne nodded. She had learned that the hard way, becoming friends with Cameron Warner. Cameron was Satan in a Dolce & Gabbana skirt. In her sixteen years growing up in New York City, Adrienne had never met anyone as manipulative and evil as Cameron.

"You should talk to Parker. Find out what's up with him," Adrienne told her friend.

"I couldn't do that," Liz said. "He'd freak."

"What then?" Adrienne asked. She slurped the last of the massive frozen chocolate drink.

"I guess I'll deal with the agony of not knowing what my boyfriend is up to the only way I know how." Liz's eyes twinkled mischievously.

Adrienne laughed and signaled the waiter over. "My friend needs a hot fudge sundae. Low on the ice cream, high on the hot fudge. We need emergency chocolate therapy here!"

Get more gossip and glamour!

"Babysitter Blues? Put the kids down for a nap and get reading!" — *Teen* magazine

Best friends Adrienne Lewis and Liz Braun have found the ideal jobs as nannies to two of New York City's wealthiest and most privileged families. Parties in penthouse apartments…weekend trips to the beach…being on the A-list at the hottest clubs…this is the lifestyle they've been dreaming of. Or so they think.

Hc 0-06-073173-7
Pb 0-06-073178-8

After months of working for the rich and famous, Adrienne and Liz are learning the hard way that behind closed doors, things are not always as innocent as they seem. Every teen has a secret—but some are way juicier than others!

Hc 0-06-073181-8

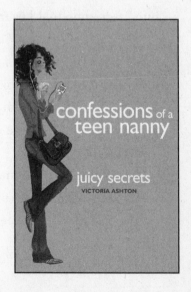

 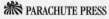